T0266367

Ariana Harwicz is an intensely passionate and fearless writer whose irresistible prose deserves to be read far and wide.
Claire-Louise Bennett, author of POND

Reading Ariana Harwicz is a raw, unforgiving, deeply unsettling experience. Her ferocious yet surgically precise sentences cut to the deepest strata of the subconscious (…). Ariana Harwicz is the real deal, the very definition of an artist.
Adam Biles, author of FEEDING TIME

The acoustic quality of her prose, the pulse of her voice, the intensity of her imagery make her subjects so daring, so relentless, so damned and unconventional – very hard to drop or ever to forget.
Lina Meruane, author of SEEING RED

The prose of Ariana Harwicz embarks on a vertiginous linguistic journey that joyfully shreds all vestiges of common sense.
María Sonia Cristoff, author of FALSE CALM

Harwicz achieves an asphyxiating writing, saturated with images of great beauty despite their disturbing character.
Isaac Rosa, El País (Spain)

We are used to female narrators who occupy one of several familiar niches (…). Harwicz takes us somewhere more profound and forces us to confront the thought that these easy fictional 'explanations' are specious. Lurking inside all of us is the potential for horror.
Hari Kunzru

FEEBLEMINDED

First published by Charco Press 2019

Charco Press Ltd., Office 59, 44-46 Morningside Road, Edinburgh
EH10 4BF

Work published with funding from the 'Sur' Translation Support Programme
of the Ministry of Foreign Affairs of Argentina / Obra editada en el marco
del Programa 'Sur' de Apoyo a las Traducciones del Ministerio de Relaciones
Exteriores de la República Argentina.

A CIP catalogue record for this book is available from the British Library.

ISBN: 9781916465602
e-book: 9781916465671

www.charcopress.com

Edited by Fionn Petch
Cover design by Pablo Font
Typeset by Laura Jones
Proofread by Fiona Mackintosh

Printed in the UK by TJ International using responsibly sourced paper and
environmentally friendly adhesive

Ariana Harwicz

FEEBLEMINDED

Translated by
Annie McDermott and Carolina Orloff

CHARCO PRESS

I

I come from nowhere. The world is a cave, a stone heart crushing you, a horizontal vertigo. The world is a moon slashed by black whips, by arrows and gunfire. How far must I dig before striking disdain, before my days burn. I could have been born with white eyes like this forest of stark pines, and yet I'm woken by volcanic ash on the garden clover. And yet my mother's pulling out clumps of hair and throwing them on the fire. The day begins, I'm a baby and my mother's in her armchair with her back to me, crying. I wake up as a girl. Outside, the lavender; inside, mother, her black hair in the embers. Cuttings of cloud everywhere, low and pasty, high and fleeting, dark and nondescript. Sitting on my clit I invent a life for myself in the clouds. I quiver, I shake, my fingers are my morphine and for that brief moment everything's fine. My hand inside is a thousand times his face inside me. How hard can you possess a face, how hard can you shove a face into your sex. For that moment, the grass is grass and I can run through the meadows. Of all the ways of being, I ended up with this one. I recognise nobody, and when I'm really desperate I live anywhere. My mother's stopped crying. I can already walk on my own, I can already speak, we already share clothes. I want him to come back against all odds, against all grief. I want his eyes to unearth me until I see the treetops. My head takes a turn. My head is in freefall, entrenched. Suddenly I have the voice of a dead woman. My face swollen like an addict in the bath, the epic body of a woman about to leap into the void. Suddenly I realise it's midday. The blue eyes of the hares shine cold and I go outside to eat, but it's already over. I begin to pray, or is it that I'm in love. I ask him to spit on me, to crush my face with a slap. I stare at him. I'm not crazy, just possessed, the answer's always the same. Mum, I'm bored. My brain is moths in a jar, hanging themselves.

My mum and the guy grab each other by the neck and rub against the slippery concrete floor. The guy comes inside my mum looking skyward and so it all begins. Let's put a microscope to my shapeless body on this afternoon thick with slow flies. People could hang it in the living room like an abstract painting. This is when the hot trees appear with their clammy leaves, and I hide from her. I hear her cry out. I'm tramping around on the hill, but where am I going. For now there's just the noise of the wind at the top and snatches of song. For now the mysticism lasts and there are ants on my arm. If you like living in a dream so much why don't you stay there, she grumbles, and shuts herself away. Without her, everything is smoke. This feverish childhood memory in a burnt-out car always comes back to me. My mother staring straight ahead, my mother on the back of my neck like a hard-shelled insect. My mother's gaze while she smokes on the train's torn fake-leather seat. Me, wide awake in the locked car, unable to speak, the neighbours calling the police. I move around tamely, where is he now. I crouch to kiss the ground. How is this possible: a relentless, niggling desire, the idiot cousin who comes to interrupt our al-fresco breakfasts of cream croissants and ends up throwing himself off the balcony. The idiot cousin who touches his nose and says nose. This epileptic desire, this deformed desire, a drooling lustful crip who needs two people to lift him and carry him like a cart so he can fuck on the soft mattress. And yet he's got nothing else to do but fuck me, but want me from his chair. And yet the clear viscous halo on the mattress is proof that I'm alive. I get my finger ready but I overthink and faint. The thought of desire on top of desire itself leaves me unhinged, a parasite with eye bags down to my neck. Where are you, Mum, I'm sick of this. I've been on my feet working for the past nine hours, the staff need a break, you know. My mum, warm, very warm, hot and now she's burnt. If she saw me like this she'd get a fright, the hatred I give off is something else. If you want to live in your dreams, suit yourself. She pokes her head out of her mousehole to insult me.

Why are we so gormless at the display counters, not knowing what to eat? Why do we use shop-bought parsley and basil when they grow in the garden anyway? And we laugh. Death a tempting option when she drops the jars of herbs and spices and we have to pick them up one by one like pieces of a skeleton, dry garlic sticking to our fingers. Lying on the sand, on the short grass, the dry soil. No more fighting my mother's arms. I try to concentrate on the taste of courgettes. They're raw, I say. Barely sautéed, she replies, just a touch of olive oil. Look at the grass, the way it's growing in patches, how strange. There are dry bits, as if only they caught the sun, and then sunken bits like marshes. A mystery, my dear, not worth worrying about. Eat up. Looks like the hens are hungry, they screech and screech. We eat. The hand goes back and forth from the mouth. Where's my phone, mum. It's not here. We said we'd do it and we're doing it really well, both of us, add a little salt. I don't ask about the thick-bottomed glasses either. Mum. He could have phoned. Concentrate. Stare at a point in space and eat up. Good idea to buy this rectangular table, wasn't it? Not too expensive, and it came with the chairs. Maybe we could do with a parasol, a sun lounger even. Yellow or stripy? It'd be nice to add a bit of colour. They say colour brings life. What crap. How about polka-dots? I'm staring at a point in space. So? Nothing exists. He's getting further away and it feels like a knife thrust in my gut. These images you fixate on are like junk food. Why don't you think about the wide-eyed, cheerful little girl you were before you met him, when you used to build hospitals for dying ants? Please don't ruin this meal. He's made you so ungrateful, you rude little hussy. I've never been cheerful. I cook from scratch instead of reheating stuff and not a word of thanks.

We clear the table surrounded by crickets. Lucky for me there's no child around, one less plate, no congealed remains, no voice cutting through mine. Nothing happening when I tear off my head with a single yank. A whiteness expands, a fog swallowing us up. It comes from back there and engulfs us, sweeping us over the plains. Chuckling, my mum remembers when my little body slipped from her hands and she was left clutching the purple cord. Everything comes back to that, to tiny knives under the water, to eels. The two of us doing the dishes with cheap washing-up liquid and gloves. The two of us putting the cutlery away in the drawers with compartments, forks with the forks, we sing, spoons with the spoons, and we do a little dance like a tarantella. The two of us go outside to drink a bottle of pastis. There's nothing. The slightest thing can bring us down: a bumblebee sting on the elbow, a glass blown over and smashed, the motionless doors and windows. One of us swings to and fro, the other sits on the bench waiting her turn. We're both in heat from the scalp down, two abandoned sows. Two foxy little sluts with bright orange muzzles. Allergic. Secretly longing for a couple of guys in wide-brimmed hats to stride through the gate, 'Can we come in?' and then they rape us over the chairs, against the wooden seesaw, in the pergola, taking one of us from behind and the daughter face-to-face. Pushing her up against the bathroom sink they stick something inside mum, the blonde guy's baseball bat. She doesn't like it much but she pretends so I think she's enjoying it. We look at each other and nothing matters. Possessing those dark, clashing eyes. They grab us by the armpits, spin us around and our long hair sweeps over the hay like a shadowy curtain. Is there any whisky left, daughter dear? It's such a relief your childhood's over, wonderful now everything's so distant it's almost like it never happened, the smell of wet eucalyptus from when you trapped your finger in the automatic door gone for good. The smell of hot tarpaulin, of rubber, of bicycle rental shops. The smell of sugared almonds, apples, pink candyfloss. I've been waiting for this moment since you were born. Did we or did we not go to the sandbanks when you turned six? Didn't we balance on the jetty? Didn't we lie along the shore, covered in sand like pieces of schnitzel, inches from the jellyfish? Is it true that when you heard a gunshot from our hotel room that day you thought it was me? Didn't we spend a whole summer sleeping under the tourists' beach canopies without them knowing, your little piles of poo like defensive walls? Those golden days, holding in my sour breath and taking you roller-skating, whole days spent helping you do headstands on the water's edge, making you jump on the trampoline, scrubbing your knickers with my fists. Hiding on the cold sand as the sun set over the beach, vomiting up your childhood.

Whisky with my mother as the electric blue fades into the small hours and now, a long way from home, my hands are covered in excrement. I didn't know my own smell, the layer of smell that forms on the body as the hours without water go by. My tongue gets distracted eating grass. Sucking on an animal's hard udders, sucking on the fur, teeth galvanised, or imagining the death of your parents. It's all the same. From the moment he entered my head, this saltwater hell. Zealous hammering on my veins. The trouble with my brain is I can't hold it back, it rolls on and on through the spiky under-growth like a bulldozer. Where am I. I don't recognise these big houses. I've never rounded this bend in the road. Degenerate desire. Damaging desire. Demented desire. I don't know how to get back. My mother will be blind drunk, sprawled on the sloping grass, her poor feet carved up by the blades. The clouds are tree trunks at this time of night, my hangover's going nowhere and I throw myself down any old how to masturbate, my hair on end, my skin hot, my eyelids rigid. My hand works away then falls still as an insect, so that nothing is enough. Me and him in a convertible. Me and him on a muddy road. Bodies shouldn't have breasts after a certain age; when my breasts turn to thick heavy flesh I'll have them removed. The sex should stop opening, too. I look for a word to replace the word. I look for a word that shows my devotion. The word that marks the spot, the distance, the very centre of my delirium. We should be like tiny snakes till the end, and be buried that way, in long holes. I get up feeling anxious, my head thick with blood. I walk round the house and open the windows. The wind sweeps over the insect corpses trapped in the mosquito net. He keeps jars back there full of rusty water and all kinds of fossils. He looks like he's never slept, always needing a wash, a new haircut, a pair of trousers with no piss stains. And after all, what is that scant pleasure we get from our fingers when we're young. What is that scant golden liquid dripping, diluting, if afterwards, later on, when at last I find her holding the thick-bottomed glass, swirling the ice cube around and asking the waiter for the same again, my mum and I are sitting at the garden table with a pot of thin broth and two spoons. What is that leftover desire, that sunken desire, while we eat our soup and the steam hits us in the face and nothing, but nothing is left.

No more whisky ever again, I say. No more whisky ever again, she says. Ever again, huh. And we make crosses with our fingers and toast ourselves with water and throw the empty bottles in the incinerator. What did I say. I want to say there's an aura of death. No. That death is all too present between my mother's mouth and mine, and in the bottom of the sunken glass. And the hours can't fix that. Starting a new day, like unplugging the refrigeration unit and plugging it back in once the storm's died down and the power's returned, and the rush to gobble up the food before it rots. But the maggot-infested cheese and the meat and entrails make us nauseous. Or mending, a whole week spent with a needle and thread, mending the holes in the mosquito nets on the window frames and painting the flower urns green. Or setting wire traps to stop the owls shitting everywhere, or throwing stones at their nests. The canary-yellow stickiness of the yolk between your pinkies. Or buying a turtle and forgetting to feed it and change the water. Wake up, mum, before the day's over, stop nodding over the scissors. She's trimmed the ends and the fringe, like every time she gets drunk. Let's go for a walk down the muddy path. Her body hunts for liquid in her organs, in the tissue around her brain. She scrubs herself with lilac-scented soap and

I watch her in the oval mirror, knowing that this pot and coffee and pills isn't the only way night can fall.

On the road, we empty ourselves out. First onto the velour seat, then onto the steering wheel. Mother onto her blue blouse with small white buttons, me down my long legs. Covered in my own waste, I had the pleasant sensation my new look suited me. We strip in the layby, our shorts tangling in our high heels. Our bras on the back seat, our guts on the tarmac, we drive off with open windows and our hair tied up. We stink as we cross the white lines, no headscarves, no lip gloss, but we're laughing for the first time in years. We never used to do that, it's not our style to drive at a hundred miles an hour howling with laughter. To want to live and laugh again. We run inside, two teenagers with sticky skin and we shower.

The phone, mum. That's enough now. We've fallen back down, back to tidying the cupboards and sweeping, the hot eggs cackling in the pan. Where is it. How do you want them? Don't make me look at you again. You're not getting it back, I won't give in. I look at the hanging baskets we put up with so much effort. I look at the tiles stuck side by side. I look at the walls and the foundations, the pieces of bread. Give it to me, now. Why do you want to leave again, we're moving on together and no thanks to old Mr Knife, the two of us alone in the old dodderers' midst. We're doing it and the day turns beautiful just like that. How about a picnic? I'll let you go on the swing. Give it to me before I overcook the eggs, before you're crying yet again in front of a cold plate of food. I should fry that fucking telephone. Give it to me right now. I should stick it in the oven. Fine, as you wish, but on your head be it, and she flounces out of the kitchen, her hands sopping wet. She enters the darkness of the corridor and returns to the light of the living room, which is dark now, in spite of everything, and she throws it straight at me.

I go outside jumping for joy. He's sent me a message and it's a shower of sparks like an ejaculation bringing me back to life. It creeps up through my body like an illness. I call him. I listen to him. He's coming. I wait at the motorway intersection, under the bridge with its far-right posters and junkies' graffiti. What is there to understand beyond this suffocation. My head is a huge flashing lamp, and now and then motors drive by at full speed. A lorry carrying a dozen carcasses of old cars. The road to the boneyard. It's been days since I last saw him. And as I occupy the anteroom, I'm a beetle on its back with fleeting pulsions pushing me into the white. Rapid pulsions pushing me into the pure. To look through a crack and see only the tree branches. The air is sweating. Horses, grass, dung, air, all covered by a single sheet. All covered by compulsion. He appears, I get in the car, we pull up outside a motel. There's nothing in between, no landscape, no motion, no succession of space time until we reach the room. Just a cut, a jump. I stay standing and my veins dilate. He unzips my trousers. I hear them fall. He turns me round, pulls down my underwear and his hand enters me like an object. With one blow the destructive force of sex obliterates my mother's blonde mane, my mother from behind, from in front, running towards me on the shore, scrubbing the salt off my swimsuit lining in the middle of a sandstorm. The times I'd board the happy train with its silly music while she'd go for her aperitif and I'd wave down at her, my head floating in the colours. The times I'd search for her among groups of women, when I'd grasp a stranger's hand. I have this monomania, how much higher can it go. Still it creeps up. While the room exists, it has the clarity of an axe.

Afterwards, if I'm not delirious, he said he had to stop coming so often. He wanted to say something but he couldn't, though he said it clearly enough when we went under the bridge and the echo sent it back. Something about his situation, the context, being responsible. That we'll still see each other, that it would be crazy not to, that I'm not in his brain so I can't understand, that I should try being in his brain just for a second, that he won't be able to drive all the way here so often. That he's risking everything. That he'll text me about when we can next meet. I listened with the reverential astonishment of a feebleminded woman getting things muddled, lost in the countless details that engulf her, a plague of microbes on the esplanade. I mistake the swishing of the animals for the plants, sunburnt lizards scuttling into the drain-pipes. By the end everything was vague, inexact, blurred. What had he just told me? We were still yoked together. My mouth an elongated snout. Where were those words coming from? Why had he chosen them and not others? What language should we use when we name things? How does anyone manage to speak at all? What had he said. I'd forgotten already. It was the thick liquid of his saliva collecting and separating in his mouth. That transition of a mouth into divinity. Like an incurable genetic condition, he finished his speech and we kissed. And kissing was a steady advance, knife raised high.

I find a note pinned to the door. 'Don't go to bed too late. Tomorrow we're going sailing.' The house is filled with snoring and it's only the two of us. I'm a spectre. I walk with my stomach scrunched up, with the devil in my guts. He falls to my feet. I move through the rooms. There's nothing, I wouldn't even say there's pain. Just these cold hard tiles underneath me. If putting your head in the tiger's mouth is no use, then what are days even for. I go round the house looking for something but I don't know what. I pace from room to room, catch a glimpse of mum shapeless in the shower, washing, marking herself up. Too late to have lived, too early to do herself in. I get into her bed without waking her. I climb on top of her and hug her to me. I'm thinning out, becoming just an idea. The idea of love for a man who lives with another, who loves another, hundreds of miles away.

I go to sleep like I'm staring into the abyss before jumping. I'm being breastfed. A mental divorce from everything and I'm no longer in this big house between my mother's legs, my mouth no longer sucking on her nipple. These old people aren't my neighbours any more, and instead I'm ejaculating all alone in the tall fresh grass. There's a roaring that doesn't come any closer. And my hand is a melodic instrument that vibrates. I'm completely unaccustomed to society, too long spent watching the mornings go by like an old goat. Fetid teeth, rancid body, skin reeking of fried onion, bacteria, badly-healed pustules. A dog tied up too many times that now growls at the sight of a baby. I can come out in support of fascism, capital punishment, the burning of Gypsies. I don't have to control my sphincter. I don't say hello or thank you. I practise remaining immobile on thorns, being cruel to the homeless, I practise absolute silence. I lounge in my basement, my office. I lock myself in and I stink. Outside, the pine trees shine and the sun is tender. Outside, other people live under low ceilings like this one, piling up rubber boots and out-of-date canned food in their wine cellars. Outside, people spend their days slumped in rocking chairs, eating fruit from tins and snoring. And they have lives just like this one, the clammy pressure of a worm in our stomach.

And crossing the corridor on my way to bed I have a vision: someone on all fours and my head reclining under twin genitalia. My wet mouth inhales that magical air, that nest. I undress, go to bed, turn out the light, in that or any other order. Mum, something's burning.

Between six and eight in the morning I swallow a strangely potent mouthful of pessimism. The people I see, the neighbour who's still alive but has a lump in his throat, below the left earlobe, mowing the lawn with the woman who keeps him company and cooks his meals, his bones getting thinner by the day. Mum's asleep. Her scoliotic back makes her an alligator. Not just the bedpan, the false teeth, all shrunken and fragile. Also the fluorescent red sunset through the olive trees or over the jet-black sea. And the purest of loves. A local couple: him with his hoof-handled walking stick, her a woman on a bicycle, easily forgotten. It's hailing, impossible to go out. Hail spiralling down, catching in the trees. Hail drilling holes in the beehives. Hail hitting the canal, the silken summer fruits, the rocks scattered along the road. Hail piercing the shiny slugs. Masturbation and lethargy. And that fatal loss. We won't go sailing, we'll stay at home and play bridge all day, play backgammon, Scrabble. Mum will develop a hunchback and the time will come when I say: I'm her. The dead woman I carry with me meanders high above, the wet ground thick with wild berries. The woman I carry parades to and fro, her trembling clit growing bigger.

I'm woken by the click click of a C11 tactical fitted with a laser. Or was it the smell of peat in the air. Or walls of stone and moss. I'm woken by a bittersweet love that's not real. Or rather than love, long, salty fingers. Traces of cowshit in the air. I'm woken by the thought that everything other than him coming in my arse just gets in the way. Mum on top of me all excited, and I just dreamt she was run over by an automatic car. The woman at the wheel wearing thick glasses and screaming from deep in her organs, how awful, again and again. I can smell petrol. They've poured some on the hornets' nest and the hens are running in frantic circles. Mum, I'm going to faint. I dreamt you were retarded, you'd mistaken me for someone else and got jealous, you kept telling the nurses I was your prince and they winked at me so I'd pretend to be him, your suitor, and you covered my beard with kisses. A tainted night, white thunder falling on bats. You're exaggerating. I'll be back soon, get out of my way, I'm off to inhale his molecules and lick my lips. That's my technique, sometimes it works. His vibration. I'm forever looking for holes to fall into. Dodging those ugly nocturnal doves. There. Let's call the doctor. The one from the knife experiment? A very cerebral awakening. You have to test your impulses: take the knife by the handle, bring it slowly towards her chest and see for yourself that you won't really stick it in. What a weird method, right mum? I was this close to slicing you open. The wind carries his smell towards me. Mother Nature brings him to the stables. Could you do me a favour and calm down? What are you on about? Motherfucking Nature won't bring you shit. Radioactive rays, pollution, that's all you'll get from her. Pure vice. Get a hold of yourself, sort out your hair and let's go. You know the moment when the sweet juice gradually collecting between your legs begins to trickle down? I want that wetness. I want that mollusc-like sloshing that keeps you from walking, that keeps you from living.

Here we are in the big, barren guest room. Swarms of flies and bluebottles echo inside it, birds with long beaks like horns, the noise of their songs overlapping. Mum delicately stretching her ash-blonde hair on the bed. Her nightdress is a robe. Are we still going sailing? The build-up of rough stones in a centuries-old house like this one, the damp from the cisterns, deafens us. Let's go to the pub. It's closed, it only opens at night. How many times do I have to tell you, alcoholics never see the light of day. Mum changes position, puts her legs back up against the wall. She seeks solace from the impossible meaning. And we laugh, we're always getting the giggles. Two sleepy loons. Let's go sailing. And we push each other out of the door, laden with equipment as if we're off to Niagara Falls. We follow the coast to the river, past cabins and steep slopes. And though we carry a stick to scare them, the hunting dogs bark at us all the way. Ever since a dog bit mum on the arse when she was out on her bike she clings to me as we walk. We untie a plastic raft, climb aboard and set off down the river. Rowing through the foam, battling the turbulence. We sail under Romanesque bridges and along the banks of medieval towns, we pass churches in the thick hot rain. For hours we do nothing but let ourselves be engulfed.

The river has burst its banks and mum's afraid, the air growing murkier and murkier. Suddenly there are waves, hollows, whirlpools, we don't know how to move in the river, how to read it, we're rowing in opposite directions. The wind pulls us to one bank and the raft gets stuck in the tender earth. Mum has fainted. I could leave her to drown and go home, call 911 from the petrol station payphone come midnight and explain how I lost her when the water level rose. Then they'll wrap me in a grey blanket to take my statement, my fingerprints, and I'll cry on some criminal's shoulder. Or I could help her climb out. We shelter on a round island, huddle on a patch of wet earth until the urge comes to undress and we run pell-mell through the woods, chased by the sound of buzzing. We cross the plains like two islands in a green sea and at one point I see her crouch down in the undergrowth, tribal.

Mum asleep with hypothermia under the blankets and hot water bottles. If her temperature goes up, 911. If she has an epileptic fit, helicopter. If she dies tonight, burial. I'm sitting on the blue chair facing the fence. On the table, a plate with some cheese and quince jelly. Mourning begins while she's still alive. The local cats and parrots have fallen silent. Gradually the childhood stenches return like potions, a hunting trail with huge trees, fragrant wood, conical or vertical canopies. Antique shops, greenhouses, mills on building sites, holiday homes, a tunnel dug with rusty spades in a grove of cedars. Everything always covered in mould. Everything always: fungus, corrosion, rust. Mum sitting me on her shoulders so I can eat straight from the tree, mummy making me walk along a fallen trunk, showing me her sex, waiting impatiently until I'm addicted. Eager for me to gain height, measuring me with a pencil against the wall. Mum delighted when my back's finally strapped by my very first bra and already I'm talking dirty. Mum beaming the day a man followed me through the woods saying, don't be afraid. The day a man followed me up the spiral staircase promising a photo of her as a baby. Mum gloating when I started drawing erect penises on the desks at school. Desperate to smoke like two chimneys at sunset, to go drinking in a pub full of tattooed sailors and giggle at the bar like two hysterical small-town girls as we feel their biceps. To go to the urinals and fantasise shamelessly. To dance a bolero pressed up tight against me without worrying the authorities will come after her again, that she'll have to pick me up later, hanging her head. Trying hard to sound measured like the other women at the police station. These summer days are so long, aren't they? Winter will be here soon. The light lopped off with an axe at four in the afternoon. Deaths by asphyxiation. I want to throw my childhood away like those balls owls spit out, bits of tooth and brain that their tiny bodies can't digest.

I'd lock myself up with him in the gloomiest, smallest, darkest places in the world. I travel towards him all through the night like a fatal proverb. Like a thrombosis. I lose everything from the neck up. I'm full. Not full, stuffed. Not stuffed, rammed. I continue my excursion. Here are handsome men, well-proportioned, but I feel nothing. They walk past and they might as well be owls. My body stills at the sight of them. I hate the thought that mother used to be floored by hot flushes. Just like that, she'd have to stay in bed all day. Or that she'd leave me on the seesaw slathered in kiddie sunblock while she filled her mouth with his hair, strand by strand, like pythons. I hate the thought that grandma used to sleep with mother, both exuding the same smell into the same side of the mattress. Strands stuck to the pillowcase. That mum used to plait the neighbours' hair so she could pick at their dinners. Or that she'd go from village to village pretending to be a free spirit, taking cheques for her open mouth. Everyone should sleep alone, like I do, and not touch anyone except me. One morning, consumed by jealousy, by the spectres of jealousy, I wake before everyone else. It's 6 a.m. A glaring sheen of light and tiny birds on the drying laundry. The freshly polished furniture, the tablecloth free of jam stains, a material silence resting over everything. I go to the swing and spend three hours there, thinking. I'm delirious with fever, I barely touch the grass. Gliding with the legs of a lapwing, the taste of candy, a sweet hairless pussy. Thinking about that jealousy, about that burning I feel when mum touches a man. Laughs with a man. About the unbearable burning when I hear her moan like she's about to wet herself, and me waiting for her in doorways, hopping over pipes, singing songs backwards. Still swinging, I decide not to be jealous any more. I go back to that day in my childhood. Something was boiling in the pan, a stew, the head of some guy recently guillotined. Something was browning in the oven, the day I finally took control of myself. I get down, I emerge from the cloud. At twelve they call me in to wash my hands.

I check the phone and nothing, not a single message all weekend after the red room. Not a single missed call after the standing penetration, after the levitation. After the hand gripping my neck, the succulent mound. After the explosion of the impossible. The impossible itself. Nothing, I repeat; nothing, I repeat. And the phone. I stare at it, put it down. Pick it up again. Start the sequence afresh. Check, rage, worry, leave it on the ground then check again. Leave the phone face-down on the table, on the grass, pick it up and it's covered in ants, blow so they don't get inside and still nothing. The world abruptly coloured like a murky sky. It's that crucial moment when anyone with any sense decides to leave. Take a deep breath, puff out your chest and go for it. Take a deep breath, stretch your legs and open the gate. If I could only have started a new chapter elsewhere. A bit of cash, a suitcase with some clothes, a few fake papers, that's all you need. I'm not even thirty yet, still young. Greet the neighbours, nice to have known you, head for the door, say bye to mum without fearing the crack of a fired arrow. Another state, another life, another person. Learn to look round without thinking when someone calls my new name, neither female nor male. Practise my signature, change my clothes, my hair.

Tomorrow, as early as tomorrow I could be sleeping on a different mattress like a total stranger. Maybe I'll elongate my eyes. I swallow the home-made jam and walk great distances in my head. When I check again I'm scared, but there has to be something. I'm scared of saying mum when she wakes suddenly in the night. Scared of hearing daughter dear in her tremulous voice. A downpour and it's the small hours again and I'm naked in the paddling pool, mum celebrating my two emerging tits. I'd finished dinner aged twelve and against the sky were aerials, wings, whistles. I stepped out to see the darkness, to slice my arms through it. Wanting to extract sap, nectar, and with my hands on my unclothed body everything was so utterly beautiful, so utterly new, the electricity falling on the water and leaving me alone. It was the first time I masturbated out of fear. Then I saw her. She'd been crouching down in her fur coat. Her cigarette was out but she was ashing it anyway. Like a capybara not wanting to be seen and becoming grass. She started to applaud, louder and louder, the perversion of love. Good girl, bravo, you're the light at the end of the tunnel, well done, you're a hot sexy bitch now, bravo, you're one hell of a woman. I covered myself up and ran away.

With the summer on top of me, I open one eye in the depths of the night. Here and now, darkness and infernal sun. The house works like a warm nightmare. I swallow half a pill. Walk with wide, hideous eyes, spin around like a goat to search for her from every angle. Her silk sheets are mysteriously cold, her wigs all hanging up, her heels in order, her dresses pressed. I have that bitterness in my mouth, the treacherous taste of life. I lose my footing. There's no solution to be found, nothing but the thirst for a bloodbath. Potions are just baited hooks. Everything out of control. Yesterday and even right now as I watch the fields open out, everything becomes a memory, a burnt breeze. Everything an archipelago. In my house there are mice in jars of formaldehyde. Mum picks them up with a spade and shoves them with a thick-bristled brush. Places them in jars with her own hands. God knows where she got a prescription for formaldehyde, but she injects them and then marvels when she sees how the organs and viscera have become a rigid little body. Look at this baby rat, it's as hard as a rock. What would happen if we took a couple of spoonfuls ourselves? We'd have to inject formaldehyde into the carotid and draw blood from the jugular while we were still alive, anaesthetised or something, right? Are you saying we could choose

33

how we were embalmed? Mum's not in the bathroom, she's not parting her hair on the swing, not reading a chintzy home décor magazine in the kitchen or drinking decaf coffee in the corridor. Each hole is packed with twisted twigs, maybe that's what did it. I'm just a few years old and mum looks at my teeth and brushes till they bleed. I'm a bit older and mum builds me a roofless little cabin among the snakes. I can't climb into my own chair and already I catch her on all fours. There are bugs in her room, recent arrivals, bugs resistant to heat. They bite our faces, our hands. We don't know what they are, so we buy something that produces a poisonous mist. The man in the shop said to flip the mattress and take all our clothes out of the wardrobe. I'll do just that, I say, arranging mother's jars and medicines in a row. As long as something's boiling in the pan, I'll close the windows and doors and let it spread. Where the hell is she. There's a trembling in the underbrush. I have to go out and look after my plant, I have to protect my nest. Even then you could see what kind of a mother she'd be, you could see her striding up the hill with her baby on her back. Learning accidentally at three months if it's a girl or a boy, learning accidentally if it has a birth defect. I wonder whether she was just pretending to be pregnant while I was inside her, whether deep down she thought all she was carrying was an almond. I grab the torch, soak myself in insect repellent and head out to look for her. Later, we'll have cold hare for dinner and it'll stick to the back of our throats. Later, greasy cutlery in the dishwasher, and dawn once more. But then a Sunday comes when we smoke in an open field, pheasants laid out around us by hunters.

I follow the main road, unsure whether to carry on straight to the curve of the riverbank, cross the wasteland towards the cottage where the shepherds live and then over the tarmac to the light aircraft hangar. It's that or visit the guy who watches the pig until its brains are blown out. Mum's left no trace. I walk away from the house and stride over the plains like a militiawoman with leather braces and enough ammunition to take down a regiment. Mum will be feeding on plants, munching them down one by one, her mouth never empty. I smile. She'll be skipping along. I'm enveloped by a cloud of aquatic insects, pyres of bees. Surrounded by bacteria. I stand there wanting to tear it all down with one sharp hack at the stem. Sweating, oozing, watching a great trunk falling towards me. The torch flickers. I step back and the metal blade pulls me low. I could hack everything to pieces with my tongue of steel. And I run, run like a furious Viking, like a purification, wielding my knife in a frenzy. I slit things open, rip out the roots that cling to the fragile soil, slash through the branches, the air. I dive into a well of bubbling water, a sauna in the middle of the hill. Mum, I'm dripping, I'm sprouting, and it's a battle with a jaguar. Gradually the dead wood from each tree begins to crumble and only the grasses and thickets are left. She's not here either, not out in the open or nestled in the shade like magic mushrooms. It's always the same, her in hiding and the little girl led by the hand of a strange man who caresses her veins. Mummy, mummy, I go from house to house asking. Mummy, mummy, I ask in the shops. Always the same performance. Mum throws open the window, makes frantic noises, but in the end she's alive and I'm left shaking for days. She and her simulations. Me naked or in my pink knickers. I return defeated through the trenches, speed up, skid. I still haven't seen anyone, and the so-called day is emerging into view. White trees. Hills. White trees. Hills, more hills, white trees. Maybe she's waiting for me with freshly baked bread and pots of home-made jam. With an apron and clear bright words. And the sky's full of flying saucers. I have no idea if these are all different forest species, if they produce pulp or fruit, if they're exotic, if they're palms, pines, vines, bays or poplars. I give no thought to the origins of the world or to learning the proper names for things. A light aircraft takes off. Two men stuff their skin with splinters, collect eggs, feed insects. Where the hell is she. Why is the day still happening. On my way back I make out two legs under the bridge, like half of a shorn baby goat. I move closer, she looks at me then walks off to finish filling the lake from her vulva. Under the bridge we scream a vowel so it echoes. Hordes of blonde daughters and mothers running to meet each other. A kaleidoscope of daughters and mothers.

II

My performance at work is atrocious this morning, and that's a direct quote from my supervisor. Are you completely blind? Has your brain stopped working or what? Where are those words coming from? I make for the car park, forgetting to change out of my uniform. I can't find my car. It's grey like all the others. I can't see it anywhere. Like when mum and grandma couldn't find me at the campsite and I had to spend all night sleeping among the lambs, their eyes bewildering balls. I go into the supermarket and have an image of the two of us running as fast as we can. Why is this coming back to me now, why this and not something else? Him and me walking on rocky ground. Every two or three stones, we stop to kiss. I see him but I don't see the car. What make was it? I see his tongue. Was there a sticker on the windscreen? I stand facing the cones dazed at the till. Not one child seems intrigued by the parcels. Bunch of ignorant peasants. Slobbering kids hanging off their mother's hands. Kids already dead in their school photos. I hear my name over the loudspeakers. Madam. Madam, they call me. I have to report to the supervisor, there'll be disciplinary action. I'm a product in the sale. I'm the old woman who comes to stroll among the Christmassy boxes. People approach me as I'm held in the supermarket, my uniform still on. They ask me how much things cost and I'm trotting through the car park, trotting and jumping from car roof to car roof.

I plan how I'll turn him on. I focus on him. I'm befuddled by the dirty hand, agitated, my antennae erect. In a trance, face distorted, I fall further. She senses something odd from the vegetable patch, her hands delving among the roots. She can't believe her eyes. What are you doing back here at this hour? Haven't you had enough time off? You're unbelievable. A housewife again with the salad and beetroot and the look of a good little matron. Get up from there, get up right now. The dilute awareness of childhood. It's all there in those precocious experiences, those glorious summers. We'd fish in dry streambeds and starve till we found a guy with a rod late at night, and then she'd get us dinner. Before that, I'd go from village to village with a rumbling stomach, sitting on the steps of chapels with my legs wide open, spitting SOS messages onto the ground. Or stealing bread from the rubbish bins. Mother from door to door. Mother with wooden heels on her clogs. And me asleep, my face buried in spaghetti or tinned tuna. Me asleep, drooling on the tables of the taverns where they'd dance with their pelvises and smoke cigarettes without filters. Stop wasting your time. She punches me in the chest to wake me. Did they send you home? It's not school, mum. What did they say this time? Tell me exactly what you've done,

I'll call them, put the supervisor on and I'll explain. Were you punished? I climb onto the crest of my desire. Up there, high in the control tower, nothing can interfere. She's talking to herself, soporific, saying jobs mean bread on the table, salt on the table, jobs keep us all sane, and I smile on through my fixation. Here she comes, rubbing her hands on the apron, and I have him on top of me, splayed out, sniffing me all over. When was the last time you got laid, mum? You're so vulgar, you're such a pig, and she treats herself to a vicious-sounding slap on my cheek. That falling-in-love feeling when they stick it right inside you, mum. The rush of joy when they ram it in deep and pull it out but then enter you again, like they're rescuing you from a swamp. Yes, that's it, he thrusts his cock inside me and pulls it out but then he comes back, comes back and I'm afloat. That saying about being cradled in his arms, but here on the other side of sex the saying is endless too. Cacophonic. Mum, you need the rapture of sex. The racing veins of sex. The stabbing, fanatical gestures, the last keys on the piano. None of that prayer and meditation bullshit. Mum rears up with her nails. She skins me like I'm a Chinese dog in a pound on the outskirts. The terror of ending up with nothing. If our power's cut off, what are we going to do. And the gas? And the freezing mornings without heating? What about having rabbit in mustard sauce from time to time, followed by a nice little cocktail in a fancy bar? And what about leather shoes, cute handbags? Judging by how quickly my grandparents and great-grandparents died, she and I will get there before long. We'll die young and sexy, we'll be the prettiest in the morgue. And there it is again, a slap on the same cheek. She drags me along by the legs, yanks me through the grass. I'm no longer in this world but another, and it's bluer, so much bluer, like the sky. Endless, celestial. Heavenly. The world of desperate thrusting, of idiotic purring. The flagrant world of sex against garage doors. See? I've learnt my lesson. She's mighty strong but can barely shake me. Agitated, she bends double, asthmatic, she can't make me react any more. And I despise this life where in the kitchen at a certain time of day the water starts to boil.

Something's biting my face. There's no space left inside me. Mum smothers me in goodnight kisses, the child in the womb like a bundle in a washing machine. It starts to lose shape very slowly, the baby tearing itself apart, its appearance fading, you were in here, she says, sticking out her belly, right here, come and touch. You consumed me to the bone. Her hair is combed back and it looks gorgeous, she's glowing from having made me. But I can see her losing energy, an old lady who makes it out to the rubbish bin gasping for air. Tomorrow I'll get you up early and take you. My mind can hold objects high in the air, suddenly I realise the ceiling's very far away. I show mum my hands against the light. They're beautiful. We'll make it all happen, she says, and rubs cream into them, finger by finger, crease by crease. Tomorrow morning we'll sort it out, I'll make you a proper cooked breakfast. Good night, she tucks me in, a pat on the forehead from the blonde with no morals. With the fairy tale of the wolf and stones instead of baby goats, or the one with cows burnt at stakes, vaccinated, castrated, wormed. And yet all I think about as I hear her get into bed is a snowy night in the countryside. Night, snow falling slowly, out in the countryside. I don't know why.

German sausages, French toast, scrambled eggs, ground cinnamon, all crispy and covered in pepper. I take my time, lazing between the sheets, but she doesn't mind. She goes with me to the bathroom, turns on the light and sits me on the toilet, my little legs dangling. She looks amazing this morning with her plait wound into a bun, her pearl necklace and her full-skirted dress. She spritzes pine-scented perfume, adjusts my blouse, buckles my sandals. Looks for easy listening, summer hits. We croon our way through the synthetic-wood factories, the industrial parks with their wholesale toys, the garden centres selling outdoor furniture, stainless-steel watering cans and large clay pots. We leave the car in the empty car park next to a heap of old shopping trolleys, she takes me for a walk and uses me as a pet. When she tries to hold my hand, I shake her off. She's nervous. She's taking me to my acrobatic dance exam and she knows I'll fall during the triple somersault on the balance beam. When it happens, she closes her eyes. It's ok, it's over, and I take two steps forward but she takes two strides back. I'll go in with you, I'll say it's all my fault, who cares. And in she goes. I try to distance myself, pretending she's a customer, and head straight for the changing rooms. She smiles at everyone and approaches the counter. The staff and the manager realise it's my mother before she's even opened her mouth. I go into the tiny cubicle, lock the door, undress. I can still smell her. My mum's precise scent. I get changed quickly and throw open the door. Some customers are already admiring their reflections in the mirrors, drifting about with hangers in their hands. A signal from the counter. It's official: mum's being a nuisance with her justifications and verbal tics, they want to get rid of her but they don't know how. Mum gesticulates. She swishes her hair back, rests her cleavage on the counter, believing she's victorious, believing she's a sophisticated woman. A customer attaches herself to me and we walk along like a pair of leeches. Mum observes my whole conversation about sizes, prices and fabrics with satisfaction. Taking pleasure in my suffering. I lead her towards the metal detectors, give her a push and watch as she leaves, her handbag swinging. She sits in the car to wait for me, the sun shining right in her face.

Several times I brush my hair out of my eyes, shaking off the drowsiness among the tall mirrors in the changing rooms. Several times a day the sky is too bright, too dazed, and she's always sitting there with the front seat as far back as it'll go. Through the window, I see her go into the supermarket and come out with a can of something and a sandwich. But during the afternoon her heavy neck of pearls slips backwards, a casualty burnt to a crisp. Later, the car park's full and some of the staff stare through the window as she sleeps or drools. I'm still on my feet, going endlessly back and forth from the room to see if the red message light has come on. I'm intercepted. Why do I take so long in the toilet, I should be serving the customers, replacing stock, making myself available. Mum dead under the sun and me trapped in this grey metal box. Mum decomposing in shades of pink and me stuck in this fridge. Mum nothing but pearls bouncing through the car park like marbles. I begin to hear the piano. If he doesn't write in the next minute, I'll throw myself down on the carpet. If he doesn't write before I leave, I'll claw a gash in my skin. There's not long to go now but my fingers are unbuttoning anyway. Half my body is out and everyone's looking. They come closer. Before they can touch me, I make for the tiny torture chamber and snatch up my phone. The use of personal communication devices is not allowed during working hours. The others look at me pityingly: a feebleminded woman who's come to get rid of her foetus. They stare at me with false understanding. Your shift isn't over yet. You're practically naked. And I leave. I throw myself through the blades of the automatic door, and I run. I run like an athlete thirsty for medals. I run over the sizzling concrete like a sprinter with new legs. I run and let evil pour out of me.

Without warning she pulls over, her eyes on me. I know she'd have stabbed me with a knitting needle if her face and mouth weren't so dry. These could be her last minutes, so I hug her tight. What did you do, you idiot, and she pushes me back into my seat. I stick my foot in the glove compartment and fill it with dirt. I got rid of them, what's wrong with that? What do you mean, what's wrong with that? What are we going to do now? They say you can't use the phone during working hours. You could always find a job yourself, you know. If she gets angry in a confined space it can be dangerous, so I dive through the passenger door when she comes at me. She gets out as well. She needs water. A whole tank of it. I try to drip some boiling hot Coca-Cola onto her lips. Why not swallow some saliva. I don't have any. Build some up, don't you know how to do that? You wouldn't survive in the desert for more than a minute. Why the fuck would I want to survive in the desert for more than a minute? Can you imagine me in the desert? She tries to fan herself with her hands but it's no use, she slumps against the car and groans. Who's the idiot now? She stretches an arm out to give me a slap, but it's easily dodged. This is it, the rituals of childhood over once and for all and now I move like a karate champion. I'm not your slave, your little Indian smuggled from foreign lands, I say, why don't you take your CV to Mr Buffalo or Go Sport. Or Tao Chi, the new venture in the Chinese district, you'll get to wear knee-high boots with red laces and you don't even need to speak English. A free lunch for two on your birthday. I can't wear boots with laces, and she bursts into tears. I move closer. Don't be afraid, mum, we don't need much to live on here, we've got land, we've got water, we've got vegetables and natural light, what more could we ask for? Two failed Bedouins. Whisky? Oysters? A convertible? Her parched face doesn't let me answer. The face of a zealous alcoholic, of someone caught in between, body tingling with desire, granted neither death nor satisfaction. She's still sobbing onto my shoulder blade and I get cramp. We'll carry on living. But how? We're drowning in unpaid bills and they won't take you on at another shop around here. What will we do, how will I drink, where will it end. A gang of motorbikes fills the roundabout up ahead.

The hyenas run around and we look at each other, our feet hidden in the overgrown green. The call from the pack to close in. Look how they're tugging at the little one's nose, these hyenas are so sick. Can't we throw something at them from here? This stinks, mum says, looking towards the forest, and she goes to sit on the swing. What do you want to throw at them? A Molotov cocktail? How much cash do we have left? She's already forgotten the baby animal. So easily distracted. She doesn't even see the remains as they're spread across the farm. I'm not a bank, I'm not a fucking ATM. Mum pulls a sorrowful face and I imagine stroking it. They always find a way to get you, these women with long, straight, clean-smelling, usually honey-coloured hair. They can say the most horrendous things, behave like utter despots, but afterwards you still want to run your fingers through the strands. How much is left, how long can we survive? We could live for decades without that filthy salary you used to waste in the ready-meal aisles. I'm not about to start cooking at my age, get old before my time, I'd rather have the pill box with the magic tablet inside. If we'd carried on eating those plastic containers, we'd have burst. How much is left, it's not a hard question for a sharp girl like you. I walk away and she follows. If I were to stop with no warning, I always think, she'd break her teeth. I empty the handbags, the pockets, the little jewellery box of banknotes. She sits on the bed and counts, sorting by colour, the big coins to one side. Counts again. Moistens the notes, her tongue turning green, turning pink. I see the breeze juggling with the air behind the thick glass. Her hands fall off, her fingers split. We haven't even got three thousand. Either we eat or we fill up the tank. I'm not selling anything, I couldn't possibly get rid of my mother's dresses, she tells me. Snivelling a little, though she tries not to. They're hand-embroidered, she was fifteen, she made them by candlelight. Oh, so now she adores her bitch of a mother. Now she'll go soppy over some scraps of embroidery. I leave before her teardrop hits the mattress. Where are you off to, she comes galloping behind me. I dial the secret number, start walking away as it rings. My life hanging from a pathetic thread. He answers in a low voice from inside a cube just as mum's jaws clamp down on my leg. I'm in a meeting with a client who represents forty per cent of our annual turnover, I was thinking about you. What use is it to me that you're thinking about me? Does anyone understand men's depraved logic? I was going to write to you. What use is it to me that you were going to write to me? Is that a joke? I was going to say I missed you, the client's watching me out of the corner of his eye, his investments represent the financial stability of… What use is it to me that…? I need to see you today, I've been fired and I'm wearing a very pretty pair of knickers. Today's impossible, what do they smell like? I need to see you today, your clients will be neatly filed away in their client graves and my knickers will be buried up my crack. Just for a bit, not more than two hours, I can't be late, my tongue licking your crack, my finger sliding into your tiny arse, tonight I have to pick up… I end the call, picturing the clients' widows laying their foul flowers of memory. The pitiful tear of the farewell ceremony, the suit, the gesture, the speech about how he's gone to a better place. Mum appears, tangled in the cord of an old iron. I'm going to get this pigsty ship-shape, she announces, her hair pulled back. It's about time we made it a home. Oh, are you going out? I'll be back in a few hours. Dinner will be ready and waiting for you, and she turns and walks away. Mimicking the gait of a well-trained housewife, although of course that's what she is. The sixty minutes before I see him are beautifully sordid, like diving head-first into a ravine.

I don't think I've ever really thought about anything my whole life. I kick stones along the side of the road. Now I'm a mass of nocturnal birds. Now I'm an impossible horrible wonderful night. Now, a hollow avalanche. People return home after chattering away in government offices or take trains out of the city, leaving newspapers rolled into tubes on the seats. I make the slight head movement that represents a greeting. A driver offers me a ride. We exchange two or three words. Like those cars in my childhood, men inside touching themselves as they ask for directions to the level crossing. That befuddled movement. Mum's womb gestated mourning, nurtured mourning, produced a carnivorous plant and now here I am looking luscious in my shorts and tight t-shirt. Though amnesiac without him, purged. Men waste so much time while they're sleeping and washing their feet. I think about my mum's sex and the man's screwed together, turning me into a little girl. I think about our hairy sexes inventing sons and daughters. There goes a mother with her hands behind her back. There goes another, biting her child's neck. The clouds can't rescue me today, they can't hoover me up. Less than five minutes to go now. How can this be described. Less than three minutes. A car passes. The wind brings respite to the troops. It can't. Here he comes. He's getting closer. And it's like letting go of heavy suitcases after a long journey, watching my fingers throb.

There you are, thank God, she shrieks. I thought you'd ridden off into the sunset with your knight in shining armour. Judging by the tired look on your face, you had a good time. Well, you both did, I don't mean you had a good time in bed on your own, but still, you could have spared a thought for me, you know, you scratch my back and I'll scratch yours and all that. We weren't in bed. And what's all this? Are we packing up and moving to a castle? Well, where do you do it, then? Don't tell me it was in that abandoned animal pen. Can't you think of anywhere better than an animal pen or a bed? Well, there's the stables, but they're filthy, all smeared with nasal and anal fluids from birthing seasons gone by. Plus you're in full view of all the farm labourers and builders, I don't recommend it, I'm telling you this for a reason. I doubt the place has got much cleaner in the past twenty years. What's that? Surprised your mother slept around too? I'd roll in the hay and come back smelling foul, my face stretched tight. And I'd run and hide from your grandma in the cart, or throw myself down on the bed, just as I was, to relive it all. I don't want to talk about it, what's this pile of stuff by the door? When you take a look inside, you'll faint. I think it's the first time in my life I've read the label on a cleaning product. I always thought detergent and disinfectant were the same, but it turns out they're nothing of the sort. I learnt all kinds of things while you were away, and I bet you did too. Ok, I'm not asking for details, positions, number of times… I'm happy knowing it was good. You won't believe me but I actually enjoyed cleaning like a madwoman. Have you been necking the bleach or what, mum? Hoovering has its moments, you know, sweeping too, it can dislodge a lot of congealed thoughts. Alienation is lovely, I fully endorse it! I tidied up your shorts, put them in order of how good they look on you. As soon as we can, we'll go to the shops and buy you some underwired bras. The ones you have at the moment are so tatty; between you and me, they give you droopy boobs. Hoist them up to your neck and squish them together so they look like one long tit. If I were good with my hands I'd make some for you. You're rambling, let me through, it'll be hard to get in with all this in the way, excuse me. I'm putting things up for sale tomorrow. I'm sure I'll find buyers in Villechaud or Bohème. You can tell by the kinds of swimming pools and security gates they have, and there's gravel in all the driveways. Automatic gates, mostly. You can tell they're classy families by the breed of their dogs. I like stopping when I'm on my bike and saying hello to the gardener, the owner of the house, exchanging a few words, how've you been, mister. I've made some dinner for you, not a drop of mayonnaise. Mum, is it just me or are you a bit tipsy? You've been talking non-stop since I got back. I've had two cups of tea, that's all. Then I lay down on the mint to meditate and listen to the cockerel – by the way, the cockerel actually says something when he crows, you pay attention tomorrow. Go to bed, mum. When all's said and done, like when you finally stumble out of the casino, don't you think sex is disgusting? It doesn't let you meditate, not during or before, let alone after. You're telling me it was just tea. Yes, cinnamon and green apple tea, while I was lying in the mint patch, and I was thinking, you know, I was actually thinking. Want to hear what I was thinking about? About a golden island, someone smiling at me from the water, everything rotting around me. I can see the scaly tails of the fish thrashing on the hot sand.

First weekday without working in a decade. I stay inside the feather mattress drinking flat Coca-Cola. Something's swallowing my heart, something's crashing against it. I can't say it was her leaving first thing, the car bursting at the seams. It's not him either, the following day I'll get my fix. What, then. I read the sky like biblical prayers. I see myself squashed, face-down, flat out in the scum. I'm not hungry, not sleepy, I don't feel like fucking. I'm not cold, not disgusted, don't want to be inside another body, and yet something is swallowing my heart. I saw mother reversing, the windscreen a clutter of objects. Wish me luck, she shouted, elbow sticking out, *merde,* like she's waiting backstage, and she was off, the exhaust pipe askew. The carbon monoxide forming shapes. I try not to think about her coming back, hair sweaty and tousled, mascara smudged, drinking to dull the failure. Money, darling, we need money, she said before going to sleep. Money, yes, and keeping on top of things and gracefully avoiding our taxes, which we don't know how to do. And bribing the neighbours so they don't go to the police with morbid allegations about the mother-daughter combo. Opening the door to them in a negligée, clumsy finger resting on lower lip, those were good times. A bunch of useless women like widows who can't even sign a cheque. I'd love to levitate an inch off the ground. Not to reach spiritual heights, absolute happiness, Olympus. To be weightless, to feel myself coming undone. Just one afternoon, an inch off the ground. It's not self-hatred, saying why did I have to come into this world, that's so easy, a stray bullet in my ear, a bullet in my ankle, mum and I spending our time hitting each other's arms and legs, raising the stakes as we get closer to the chest and ending near the grassy mound, our private female cemetery with no brain matter. Mother would play happily after dinner, beer with lemon and olives as a farewell. Dissipating in the afternoon, that's where my mind was when I heard the first screams of panic.

You're swallowing your words, I can't understand a thing. She's screaming at me from the car. What happened. The car a rubbish tip and mother shrieking, clutching the steering wheel. They might follow me all the way here, we have to leave. Why, where. I manage to open the door and get her out. Her make-up's smeared and she's having trouble breathing. He invited me in, a little house, nothing fancy, but well looked-after, between the other grander houses on the hill. He invited me in, I wanted to show him what I had, offer him good deals, but he insisted we have a drink first. Why do you get into these situations. We're in front of the park, it's the time when kids come out to play and people are doing exercises, hanging from those bars that tone your abs. Get to the point! Don't rush me! But you're never able to get to the point! Well, I went in and this unprepossessing guy closed the blinds and threw himself on top of me! I'd swear he wanted to have his way with me right there on the table. You could swear or you do swear? He hurt me. He tried to grab my feet but I ran, I ran all around the house looking for a way out and then I ran through the back door. Look, I'm covered in bruises. I thought the car wasn't going to start, I swear. I had to put the key in and turn it ten times. Define unprepossessing for me.

You just repeat stuff you hear without thinking, and you never get it right. Are you mocking me? And what did this unprepossessing guy want? To kill me, what else, are you a half-wit? But why would he want to kill you. It doesn't matter, he wanted to kill me and that's that. There doesn't have to be a reason. Are there reasons to rape someone doggy-style on a table and then hack them to bits, put them in a bin bag and leave them by the roadside till the rubbish truck comes by. Honestly, I swear, I don't understand you. I brought you up so naïve, I raised you so badly. I lowered you, more like. Can you please stop swearing things and messing around with words? Did you sell anything? No one had any cash on them. Let's bring the stuff inside and you can have a nice long bath, soak in the bubbles. Forget the sales. Neither of us has the soul of a saleswoman. Neither of us has a soul. Let's dig an organic plot. Oh, because we have such green fingers, I can see it now, everything planted upside-down. It was a good idea, I still think it could work if we did it properly. The guy had a pot in his room that smelt of stale cat, would you believe, the things people do when they're lonely. In silence, we take the stuff inside and tidy it away. We cook pasta with walnut oil and eat dinner covered in mosquito repellent. Mum smokes as she digests the spaghetti, holding an uneaten piece of bread in her hand the way old people do. We're born to chew on resentment, at times like this I want to see the world end, she sighs, and maybe that's the key, let the world end and everything will begin again. And why would everything begin again? And why not? No, the question is why would it. The question is why the fuck would everything begin again? To make it all less terrifying. Don't you realise that this guy everyone took for a monk could have finished me off with one blow?

Let's go over some self-defence techniques. Life's a bitch on heat but sometimes it offers the unthinkable. It offers me a diabolical purity. It offers me him. Huh? What the hell has that got to do with anything. You enter the woods, daughter dear. I love him all the way to howling like some bristly beast. Let's go over the techniques. I enter the woods. You enter the woods. I walk along calmly until I see the caravan and the old man, naked. Outside, pans and oil drums. Outside, the dregs of dirty starry nights. And an army uniform. Degenerate old man. Let's not judge him so quickly. I see him naked, sunburned skin, varicose veins, flaccid flesh. An old man. Maybe the last surviving hippy, a paedo-phile, a compulsive gambler. Perhaps a fugitive, an illegal alien. Or a granddad with dementia who left his garden to go fishing one day ten years ago and no one came looking for him. It happens. Does he have an erection? Not yet. I walk past him, pretending not to look, like one of those women out for a run, or I stare at the pond with the raft in it, or at the leaves that float like oars. Does he get hard? No, mum, he just gazes straight at me. Is he an immigrant? Don't be racist! Then don't be an idiot. Well? Yes, he gets hard. There's something jagged in his hand and on the tip of his tongue. The spikes of his unshaven beard. The wind's blowing hard. It doesn't blow us, it inhales us. And what do you do? What do I do. You hit him on the neck, a sharp chop, right where there's no muscle tissue. A solid blow. Or you stab him in the eyes with both thumbs, really deep. Or you go for the balls. Neck, eyes, balls. Right. And then I look for a flat stone to hit him with, quick. On the temple. Hit him on the temple before he sees you've picked up the stone, you've got to move fast. You can't miss. And then I run. As fast as you can, away from the undergrowth. You don't hide in the mill, or the caravan next door. You run all the way across and step right into the house where the hungry shepherds are waiting.

Just now I dreamt he was about to escape in a truck. I found the key. Hallelujah. Wake up. We don't need the Apocalypse any more, there's something even better. Mum, stop shaking me or I'll kill you, I swear. Fine, fine, but get up, I'll put the kettle on, I'll make some toast then I'll tell you. What's the time. There's no time of day when there's light in the sky. What are you on about, Jesus fucking Christ, someone take this woman away. Up, get up. Time doesn't exist after sleep. What the hell are you saying? I saw him in that delivery lorry covered in soil like tentacles, going down an iridescent mountain path. I'm sure he was coming towards us, you can know that without knowing it, and he was getting further away, this is the main thing, he was getting further away from his family. Iridescent? He didn't care about anything, not his most important clients, not his father, not that insipid woman. He left them with a house, a car and some land – extraordinary, isn't it? – and he was coming for us, my son-in-law. Mother breathes like a fish out of a bucket. Remarkable, isn't it? Dim frequencies of icy heat cut across the room. Are you in your right mind? No, I'm serious, can you honestly say you're in your right mind? What are these questions. Why are you hurting me like this. Do you want a stamped certificate from the

Ministry of Health or something? How long has he been coming to see you. How long have you been gobbling each other up like dirty lice without stopping so much as to piss or to cough. A year and a half. Well then, a year and a half is longer than wise. Didn't you see that massive cobra eat the crocodile after struggling desperately for five hours. Well then, he should have made the leap, he should have come to you on his knees by now. No excuses. No flowers bought on the motorway. No necklaces without labels. No monosyllabic text messages. It's none of your business. This is an emergency now. And actually it is my business. Anything to do with my daughter is very much my business. You'll understand one day, if you have a daughter yourself. Meet up with him. Ask him when he's planning on leaving her, because you know what, it's very simple if he's not. Do you want to know what I think? No, please, I don't. Well, I'll tell you anyway. The question's there just to wind me up, as usual. Is he still fucking her? On a regular basis? Who starts? What positions? Always in missionary or do they mix it up? How long does it last? Who does he think of? Because all that stuff about how he's not really into it when they fuck, I don't buy it. He fucks her, he gets hard, he ejaculates and that's that. Mechanical or poetic, he gets hard and he ejaculates. And it's not fair. I launch myself at her and grab her by the neck. We fight on the bed, sheets and skins tangled. I'm never asking him that. You just want to fuck things up for me. You want him to leave me, to get sick of me so it's just the two of us again. Mum throws herself on top of me, I break free and she comes back for more. I leave the room and sit on top of the ants. I can't stand this depressing smell, an unwashed saucepan. I stumble back and open the mirrored door, knowing mum's hanging off the bed for extra drama. I stuff some clothes and other things in a bag, fill it with badly-darned socks, slippers, knickers. I sling the bag over my shoulder and the fury on an empty stomach makes my forehead thump. I'm leaving, I should have left a long time ago. No answer. I'm leaving. And I cross the dining room. Yes, unbelievably I cross it, the dining room where mother spent that long pregnant winter, where I was born among towels and dressings, where I gave my first blood-red scream on leaving her flesh, an eternity, the head finally out. I cross the kitchen where we consoled each other, where we sat and decided to bury grandma after she was hit by a car, accepting the reduction in our clan. I cross the garden, it's a miracle to be crossing the garden. Farewell to that insatiable lust of puberty, rubbing myself against the grass, farewell to giving myself to him like he's the only human on earth. I cross the garden where I used to run around talking gibberish. The garden red and black from the drama and jealousy on the day of my first kiss. Mum asking if there was any tongue, if it felt forked. Digging. Tongue how though, like a whirlwind or like a vacuum cleaner? Did you chew some gum first? But also the glowing afternoons, real as cutting your finger on a sheet of paper. Mother emptying the pot of my piss. Mother sniffing my armpit, shuddering at the taste of my sweat. I pass the twisted trees and each tree is an era, the three of us climbing, the two of us climbing, picking the raspberries and blackberries one by one from the branches before the albino-feathered blackbirds could get at them. I cross the fence like I'm a well-endowed cowboy.

III

I leave her the car. The keys in the ignition and some cash on the seat. Enough not to die of starvation for a few days. Enough to eat junk food and get hold of booze. Or to take advantage of the summer sales and pick up leggings and lycra tops in the supermarket, because she loves going through the cut-price clothes from previous seasons. It's hot and night still hasn't fallen, though it's come a little closer down the long road and the round-abouts. Cyclists pass me hunched over like rodents and I keep going. If I don't stop, not even for a second, if I don't see anyone, I'll make the nine o'clock train. No dinner but I'll make it, and get off at one of the stops, or at the end of the line. I think about him. I think of messaging, of calling. But he has to do it, it's his turn. To cheer myself up I look at the neon signs of the American meat restaurants, whole families sitting down to buffalo steaks. I reach the station just in time. I don't stop to buy a ticket, I board the train as it departs. I'm sitting down and the earth's going by. No news. I think about him. I try to wrench my mental bearing in a different direction. What will mum be up right now, is she at home or in the woods, is she still alive. But no, I can only think about him. We've passed one stop so far and I'm still here. A young guy in the seat in front turns round and asks me something. I take a while to respond and he's already looked away. The inspector is coming, I smile at him, cross my legs for him. It works. Thanks, mum. None of the stops convince me, none of the houses, the colours. I get off at the end of the line. Who knows if I'll find anywhere open, or if there'll be a hotel nearby. I'm hungry, cut off from the world and all I can think about is him. I've never – I realise as I read the sign – never been to this city or any other, except for visits to the doctor, consultations, electroshocks. I've never visited a city and been conscious when I left. But I return. He reels me in. I'd still be thinking about him if at this very moment someone were beaten to a pulp with a shovel right under my nose. I sit on the kerb and send a text: I'm alone in an unknown city. I've left home. I need you. With my bag on my back I walk down the main street, against the traffic. Amen. A light breeze, a symphony. I rest by a canal, eat in a pizzeria covered in roses opposite a cinema. And as I watch the water flow under the arch, under that precise sky, I don't think about him.

When I finish, my skull is trepanned again like a falling axe. He hasn't written. He hasn't called. He hasn't shown up. Where is he. What's he doing. With whom. I pay the bill without looking at the waiter's face. Does he even have a face? I watch them hold a stethoscope to my chest and prescribe the strongest thing they have and I sleep the whole train journey back, the chequered profile on her drool-wet skirt. It's hot in the waiting room. The kids suck pear drops, they have asthma, she fans herself with her hand. Always the same, she explains my symptoms, her symptoms, the doctor gives the order, I open my mouth. The two of us drinking hot chocolate after-wards or riding the merry-go-round to celebrate. For an indeterminate time I don't look for a hotel, I'm just nowhere. I walk along gazing at the window displays, copy shops, repair shops, dry cleaners. A whole life spent in the gloom of a shop, the iron keyring, the fuse box, the stairs to the storeroom. The tiny bathroom. The cleaning products and polishing the shelves. A whole life. The clock-in time, the sound of the shutters rolling up, rolling down, the bell every time a customer walks in or out. The changing rooms, the smoke-filled alley behind. Stepping out for a fag when the owner goes to the bank. I'm inside carrying extra weight, my bra digging in. My lunch is packed, I drink a Coke at the counter and have sexy dreams on the grass. Faced with the lady in the lobby, I don't know what to say. She waits. How many people? How many nights? The wallpaper with green flowers like spiky thorns, like knitting needles, reminds me of my mother. Of my rococo mother. Of that insipid morning marked with a cross in the kitchen calendar, when she'd get rid of the unknown creature inside her. Of the night she and grandma threw dice and luck said better to be three people at home and avoid a suspicious premature death, so they drank a toast outside with little glasses of vodka, lit the candles and roamed through the house like shadows. Of the time when the drizzle gradually became a downpour, and granny laid her down so the ghost could come out.

You don't think she's one of those lesbians, asked grandma with downturned mouth when at fifteen there still wasn't a boyfriend or a suitor in sight. And mum shot me a look that said you'd better fucking not be. I lean on the banister and peer out into the street, empty but for a Chinese restaurant. No one's gone through the door for hours. I wonder if everyone's dead in the fish tanks, if there was a bloodbath, a settling of scores. I wait to see the red come seeping under the door like an open artery. No messages. I see him with her in the toilet. I think about him so much I have no air left to imagine him. A maelstrom of resentment gathers within me as the sun comes up. That's when I see my dad's aura. Dad, what is that. I never said it like that. And I see it's a very tall young man with blonde hair who's always looking for somewhere to stick it. The day begins like it did yesterday. I eat, drink, sleep a little. A dog chews on the car tyres. Alarms go off and scatter the birds. The clumsy things squawk, slice through the sky, swoop lower, attack each other and flap on through the air above rooftops and girders. What for. Which bird is which. How to know which is in freefall, if it's this one or that. The mid-morning sun irritates my eyes. My blood burning, the dog's jaws shredding the tyres, this mattress, dad catching salmon or selling boat engines, dad dressed in leathers and smoking outside those cinemas that show sappy films, waiting for a woman, it could all be true. The only thing that gets him out of bed in the morning is the prospect of penetrating someone. Dad and mum clinking glasses of cold malt beer on their first encounter. And then another glass, and another, emptying the fridge while granny spies on them. Dad showing off his testicles up on the tractor's jib arm, dad smelling of aftershave for teenage boys, mum bored to death by that bleached-blonde six-foot-two misfit who takes her away with him to behead cobras. The same jacket and shoes several days in a row, something that fascinated my mother: his smell distilled. And they end up fucking in the arse on the sofa.

One of the three always watches the other one do it. Grandma watches mum with that beggar from the north, mum watches me with that dark-skinned guy with the silver ring, and I watch them both, one at a time, each in their bedroom as the little girl wanders through the house with a box of Coco Pops in her hand. The little girl on tiptoe trying to reach the knife. Then they do it with the showerhead, throw open the windows and sheds to let the air in, quickly fling their underwear into a bucket of water. And they sniff their fingers under the nails and kiss me euphorically, cigarette in hand. They tell each other everything, whispering the salacious details. I used to like going into their rooms to inspect, to bounce on their shifting mattresses, to find the things they'd forget under their beds. I walk through this city of reeds, palm trees and roots that crack open the streets and the patios. I've gone a whole day without hearing either of their voices and it feels like hot clouds suspended in mid-air. Pretending I had a mother who wore dresses gathered at the waist, a mother addicted to the luxury of seaside casinos, pretending there was a cowboy who came to rape me by the side of the motorway, gorging on me until I lost my bearings. The treetops are moving and they're the sand dune we used to visit, sea shells and the rough towel shared between granny, mummy and the little girl. A trio of red arses on the clams. Three chubby backs covered in sunblock. Three sandy vaginas to end the day. Finally I come to a tavern. The ham and lobsters displayed in the window are almost certainly unfit to eat, but I order them anyway. I sit at a dark table, the ashtray overflowing. I'm still dazed as I devour the menu, the waiter observing with interest. I'm dazed by the path of the sun and the shadows, in this tavern, in this city. The phone rings. I hit the button instinctively, my mouth dripping with fat.

I spit it all out right away on the kerb, the lobster falling leg by leg into the road. Trip with pink little skips to the hotel bathroom and brush my teeth, my tongue. Take a shower, stick the bar of soap right up, blow-dry my hair, become voluptuous, put on my high heels, and rush perfumed to wait for him at the entrance to the cinema. Surrendering to love. To being trapped in his hands, giddy in his air, so profoundly giddy that I can't follow the subtitles, that I find it impossible to decode any irony. What was irony again, what was decoding again. I inhabit this inner courtyard full of retards doing handicrafts, climbing on top of each other and laughing. So-and-so rode the mule, I ride the mule myself. I'm the one in the hospital photo being restrained by the man in white, and back there are the relatives who've come to visit. I'm a farmer who breeds children. There are tiny creatures floating in the pot. It lasts, the luminous fragility lasts, for as long as he doesn't leave and we walk, discover the city, eat, wrap ourselves around each other naked. That's what exists while penetration is a moonlight sonata and the rest is filth. And I don't understand but the sequence of events means it's over and we're sitting in his car near the station and he's saying something that makes the windows steam up. He's saying something but my finger's on the button and I can't hear a thing. He kisses me but he needs to talk. I kiss him but he asks me to let him talk. It's urgent. I feel my hair falling out as I hear him say she's entering the final stages of pregnancy.

What if I'm an orphan now thanks to her? What if she's lying on top of grandma with a wooden cross and a note? And if the house isn't there any more and in its place there's a gully and foxes drinking. The train back crosses Siberia in winter. My head is now bald. Why do I always have to be so stupid. When I get off I'm already running but my knee gives way and I fall. Hatred is not enough. You're going to pay for this, is not enough. His wife miscarries, the lounge streaked with bodily fluids. What a shame, now get busy with the kitchen wipes. Or she reaches forty weeks and the long-awaited day arrives, out pops the baby with its name and cot all ready and waiting but it's born dead. A minor detail. Or the scans show everything in order, the nervous system still forming, all normal, the little feet, the nuchal translucency, the involuntary foetal movements, and the amniotic fluid just gorgeous, the cervix looking fabulous, but when it comes out it's Siamese and stuck to a dog. Or it's born a healthy baby, the scream marking the animal act and then he's latched on her tits all covered in shit, the three of them back in their home sweet home with the steri- lised hospital bag, combs for delicate skin, the postnatal belt, the nasal aspirator, the whole useless arsenal and a bottle of Calpol. But one night when they're all fast asleep, she squashes him to death. It happens all the time, says the nurse. An autopsy back in the big city and then burial in a special section of the cemetery. All that's left is for her to glance at the other child graves, her breasts still leaking. Mourning with its different stages. There are no stages, just blowing yourself to bits in an open field and splattering your guts willy-nilly. Swine. Bitch. Two degenerates. How could he penetrate her, ejaculate inside her. Mum warned me. Mum knows. Mum saw the way things were going. He said it was mechanical, like eating when you're not hungry, that you can eat even when you're gagging. I'm almost there. It still looks like a house. It still has windows and walls and a chimney. I don't see any flames licking the tallest trees. The fire engine's not here with its ladder reaching all the way to the roof. No one's carrying her out on a stretcher.

I go inside shaking. At first glance, it all seems under control. But as I move through the house, the details. The gas half-on, the tea towels rolled up against the door, the windows latched shut, the bathroom tap dripping. A subtle whiff of decomposition emanating from the fridge. None of my mother's belongings in sight, no jewellery even. I'm in the middle of the waterfall and everything is silence, I'm blinded by the violent torrent. No one in the dining room, no one in the hall, no one in her room or mine. My bed made. No one in the basement surrounded by open bottles, no one on the terrace or hanging from the beams. Right. I'm an orphan, and I see myself in front of my ancestors' graves, liberated, an empowered urchin, unhinged happiness. To say, I'm an orphan, like saying I'm a married woman, or I'm hungry. Stumbling outside, smelling everything for the first time, beginning to be reborn. I walk in a straight line through the overgrown grounds, leaving the empty house behind me. As I walk I search for her high and low, looking up at the sky in case she's hanging from a parachute, dangling off the wing of a fighter plane, fluttering naked in the branches. I walk following the maternal instinct I don't have. I need a piss. Live without her. Move up a gear into panic. But she must be able to feel me, the pack licking their wounds after the hunt. Live without her for the minutes before I shoot myself. How will it feel to drag myself all the way to the marble top. How will it feel to reach the little drawer, the bullets, the holster. How will it feel assembling death. In the distance, galleries of stone and red hills. And the inert state of the puddles.

If an aviator saw us from above he'd fall out of the sky, letting his plane plunge headlong into the green chaos below. Heart hammering, lunging forward with flailing arms, I am broken apart. And it's like driving through a field of hawks, accelerating until everything's a whirlwind of flame. Wandering through space but holding fiercely to the ground, I feel her vibrations and impurities. I fall at her feet. The claws of the beast. Mother, forgive me. Forgive me for betraying you. Yes, that's exactly what it was, she says, a betrayal, and a brazen one. I know. Forgive me, mummy. Staring into each other's eyes, we're two bees suspended like objects. I don't know if I'll be able to forgive.

The truth of passion, daughter dear, is its impossibility. Oh God, mum, please, I've heard it all before. Shhh. What I'm saying is, if it were possible, it wouldn't be possible, something I learnt the day I climbed onto the bonnet with a little rucksack on my back and said to my tall blonde man, I'm coming with you, I'm your property now, I want to die in your arms, and that was the last I saw of him. So what I mean is, it's possible because it's impossible. Yes, yes, I know. Shhh. Even knowing it off by heart, that the suffering caused by the impossibility of passion is what makes it so passionate, still we fight to make it possible. Why the fuck is that? Now I'll let you speak. Shhh. Because that's what women are like, we're wicked, pig-headed creatures. We have feathers for brains. We don't want to suffer, we hate to suffer, we're terrified of our heart beating in every part of our body as we gasp for air and he tells us he's no longer in love with us, that he can't get used to our smell, some bullshit like that, and yet if we don't suffer there's no passion. Suffering is how we make possible the impossible: it's passion itself. In those few moments when the suffering – the dread of losing him, of there being another woman – disappears, and I know this very well because there were days, listen carefully now, there were days, the only days in my whole

90

dumb life, when that blonde guy would bring me gifts made with his own hands (matchboxes, painted worms, weirdly-shaped twigs), on those days he'd kiss me deeply and it seemed his slimy tongue would stick to me and lick me down to nothing. So on those days, you see, I didn't suffer at all. Whole afternoons by the lake, free of suffering. But I wasn't happy either. Falling in love is the ultimate curse. Falling in love is the downpour under an electrified roof. I don't know if you follow. I don't know if I'm making myself clear, now you're old enough. I always used to say, wait till she's out of nappies, wait till she can string a sentence together, wait till her first period, wait till her first time, before you break it to her… But in the end, I never did. Falling in love is confronting the six-foot cobra. I couldn't teach you in time. I'm so sorry. You did teach me, mum. I failed at everything, I started your childhood back to front. I should have given you a proper education, stopped you from sticking your fingers into your shell and pulling out the slug. No, mum, you're wrong, seeing you was enough. I hear her voice as I lie on the moss, a thin green layer covering me like fine sand. I'm lying down like a mammal, woolly ears over my eyes. I'm upholstered, lined, and between my mother and me runs a cliff edge, the water rising and rising.

She spends all afternoon planning our revenge. All afternoon. Bastard. Coward. Son of uncountable whores. Son of uncountable whores? Really, mum? Ok, fine, son of a bitch. And chucking bottles onto the dump by the neck, one after another, all the empties downed in my absence, I realised that we're born by mistake. Sprawled any old how in the afternoon, clumsy, weak-willed, uncomfortably full. The nurse tempted as he leans over the female stroke patient. That we're born out of weakness. Children conceived just to fill in the gaps or early one morning with no eye contact, after someone slips up, like mum just now, blitzing bottles with her sticky hands. With each mercy shot she whispers the plan to herself, how we might get rid of all this shit, how he'll lift us to safety, pull us up by his dick like a digger pulls a buried family from the rubble after a hurricane. And then, stay still dear, you've got an insect stuck to your eyelid. I get this crazy urge, mum, I want to pull out my eyes and my heart when desire makes me lose my head and my senses. Spare me the theatrics, you dirty little slut. Did he at least call you? Did he console you? Did he say I love you? Not even that. And here you are, whingeing away about pulling who knows what out of your senses. Don't worry, she'll lose it, she won't make it to nine months. I'm no harpy, I just know a thing or two. That's just what I was thinking! It'll plop out between her legs, it'll be born dead! And we celebrate the coincidence with a pretty little waltz, kicking the unborn in the head. Did he ask you if you wanted one? Coming up to thirty, it's what you'd expect. Didn't he say he'd give you one? It only takes a second to slip you some sperm like an offering, a token of gratitude at least. Oh, don't start all that again, your eyes are like strawberries, let's do something else, we'll prepare it all step by step. It'll be like watching live as the glaciers move, a seminal performance, enough of all those brainless cows on the horizon. But I'll need you for it. Go and have a wash and come back fresh-faced. Don't even think about touching the phone, I'll tell you when it's time to send the first text. You have to make them wait so they react. Off you go, and she kicked me hard on the arse. An avalanche of light and weight is tearing down everything inside me, mum. Once you've levitated, what else really matters, why bother to experience anything at all. Get a move on, right now, and don't talk so much, you get muddled up in your own words. Slash at those poisonous plants, flashing blows to their brittle hollow stems. Not enough. Bring my nose close to the soil, close to what's left of the stags' wild rutting. What am I going to do, mum? To the bathroom, right now! Are you deaf? Run through a body and come back over a storm, and on your shoulder the bundle, still warm.

Don't be afraid, don't be afraid. What are you afraid of now, hurry up, shock therapy for this one over here! He's not making a move because he's in the doghouse, he's waiting for a sign from you, it's your reaction he should be afraid of, the ball's in your court, come on. And on top of everything else, the other one's knocked up. Now there's no chance he'll touch her, not even with a wire. A bargepole, mum. Fine, wire, bargepole, whatever, call him right now. Stop driving me crazy, stop indoctrinating me, go somewhere else. I'm not indoctrinating you, I'm educating you. And I need to listen to what you say, I need to give you ideas, you can follow my lead. I don't need your ideas, get lost or I won't call him. And I step out onto the road. Mum stays inside playing solitaire on the coffee-stained table. I see her shuffling the deck, a quick lick along the tip of a card, cheating. I walk with the phone burning my hand. I walk so far I pass two deserted villages. I circle round the cemetery, the niches visible over the wall, the containers of spiked water. I'm not calling him yet. I turn around and see shops selling marble, granite, polishing and varnishing services for floors and gravestones. Cleaning and decoration services for graves. Ready to cremate the whole world. The sky seems further from the ground than ever. I search for his texts but I can't find any; she's deleted them all. I go in through the gate. Four young men are carrying a coffin. It's hot and the sweat on their hands forces them to stop. They don't seem to be thinking; it's as if they're on a mountain path, enjoying the view with binoculars. Afterwards they'll join their relatives for lunch and with every minute that goes by they'll forget they came here to bury a body. A body that used to move. They set the coffin down in the shade of a poplar. I call. I've lost track of the maternal instructions. What was the extortion about. How much was I meant to ask for. I imagine him here, I imagine carrying his weight, having to take a break so I can carry him a bit further. He answers. I can't say a word but he knows it's me. He was waiting for my call, he was anxious to know I was ok, he was concerned. He doesn't speak a word of love and the fever rises and suddenly my lips are purple and I'm her. I need to see you, at least to say goodbye. I need to believe this separation is real. He says he understands. Sure, he says, I understand. That voice of the unpossessed. Disgust. Loathing of that life about to give birth. After strangling me till I was nauseous, after thrashing like a shark and now the pitiful music of daily existence while the chambermaids clean our hotel rooms. The hungover quilts shaken out of the windows. The empty bedside tables. The hoover on the carpet. But it was that other common bitch who got him. I want to bury him. I want to dismember him. He doesn't give a day, or a place, or a time. I'm a virgin who lives with her mother in a caravan and in winter they rub together like two cetaceans. I'm the woman who eats duck liver with her fingers and broken nails. The woman who laughs and holds hands as they skip through the windstorm. Her pussy locked up until old age. And when one snowy morning she finds her mother on her back with her mouth wide open and an insect inside, she throws herself on top and starts kissing her, swallowing the insect like an ice cube. The young men leave the cemetery. Tomorrow, the killer goes free. I degrade myself. I need a hand with some bills, you know, I got sacked after ten years and it wasn't fair, it was discrimination, I'm going to sue them, you'll see, and I'll win, and with the payout I'll buy myself a yacht and go island-hopping, oh yes. But for that I need to hire a lawyer, of course, he says he understands the situation. What kind of discrimination? I don't bother answering. How much do I need, he'll get it for me. I'll pay it back as soon as I can, he knows a good lawyer and an accountant. The things a man will do to get rid of a woman. Her dead weight. He's so obvious. So reasonable and measured. Setting a date for ten days from now, putting it in the diary without batting an eyelid. He'll come and see me, but he'll have to leave early because they've got an appointment they can't put off in… I hang up. Naturally, he's now rubbing the plural in my face.

That anxious longing twisting my fingers. The meeting place is the same. Under the bridge with the anarchist graffiti and the prostitutes' phone numbers. There's no definition, this isn't waiting. It's the void until he appears. A lazy day of lactation. Mum locked up at home praying, kneeling on the floor tiles. Mum still waiting for the other guy to come. The guy who left her in flames, banging her face against the trees. The guy who'd pull it out just when she was on the brink and laugh at her, fag on lip. Mum going back over the sequence, going into the wardrobe. Mum, a final check of the blade. The first time she's conducting something, the first time she's inspired. Here he comes. Instead of switching off the engine and throwing himself at me, sucking my face off, he signals he's going to double park. I get in, follow orders and the juicy kiss comes after we go through the motions. How are you, how's your mother, what have you been up to. I brought you the money, you can count it, pay it back when you get the chance, no big deal. What utter crap. I don't reply. It's hot, he says. Finally a day of real summer, swimming pools till midnight and lazy barbecue lunches. The city has collapsed from an overdose of air-conditioning. Here, right? You couldn't put up with this heat in the city. I take the wad of notes and put it in my handbag without looking. I need you to come home and give me a hand, I have no one, it's awful. What's the matter. It's awful, two women living like this and now mum's left, I have no one. What's going on, don't scare me. A plague, all through the house but especially in the kitchen. Of ants? Of those horrendous little white rodents. That's disgusting, but what can I do, I know less about all that than you do. Help me, it's the last thing I'll ask of you. Don't you have any neighbours? What about calling the fire brigade? My neighbours are all half-dead. The fire brigade stopped coming after mum called them thirty nights in a row with different excuses, please don't make me talk about it, kittens on the roof, the boiler exploding, a baby crying in a trunk. It's their duty to come, it's a service to the nation. Mum harasses them, it's not their duty to be harassed. I'd rather go somewhere else, you know, I feel more relaxed in a neutral space, and he carried on talking but I threw myself at him and bit the inner part of his ear. And the car starts to reverse, the wheel in the gutter and it turns. We'll do it quickly, without looking, you can pick them up and I'll throw them away, I've got latex gloves. We have to hurry because otherwise they'll get into the fridge and that'll be it, they'll finish our supplies. I've never worn latex gloves before. Better than getting your hands all gooey from the baby ones. Christ. I can't, no way. I look at him and kiss his lips, gripped by that euphoria which appears out of nowhere and then vanishes for no reason. I hope you understand, he says. I'm here, but… Sure, sure. She's quite old to be a mother, I couldn't take it away from her. Not after all these years together, it would have buried her alive, yes, of course, I get it. If I left her now she wouldn't find another man, it's even too late to freeze her eggs. Her ovaries are worn out and the least I can do if I don't find her attractive is give her… Sorry to cut you off, but could you leave the car in the garage? I'd rather leave it out here, no, inside is better, otherwise the kids'll scratch it with screwdrivers or water pistols, they're not used to seeing new models like this around here. Anyway, I was saying, a person has a moral obligation to someone they've been with for so many years, I can't just throw her away like she's a thing, she's not a toy, there's no desire any more but there's no repulsion either… Sorry to interrupt again, but does it have a sliding sunroof? It does, that's what made it stand out from the other cars we saw, we both thought the transparent sliding roof was amazing. I'm sure you'll go for some wonderful drives down the coast, along the breaking waves, the little one like a mini ice-cream cone with half his body poking out. So, you get what I'm saying? You can put yourself in my shoes? Come on, over here, follow me. And quick, cover your nose with this, it stinks.

He comes in watching every step he takes, the pebbles crunching beneath him. What is it? Don't you like the modest décor? Don't you approve of our rustic ladies' idyll? No, it's not that. I just feel weird, we've never been here together. I was joking, I think the décor's revolting. Soon I'll be moving a long way away and you'll see how I decorate my house then. Oh, really? You're moving to the city? I have some plans. Well, let me know, I'll help you find work. Mum's not here, don't worry, I won't do the official introduction today. Come in, come in. Take off your shoes, you can leave them in the pile with the others. He takes them off, goes to the bathroom, I realise he's taking a moment to think at the mirror with the water running. Every drop is a trap. I'm thinking too. I'm figuring out a plan B in case he escapes through the window. The house is well-equipped, there are wires, nets, shovels, even an old tractor. I wait right outside the door, I pounce. And the family of little white rats? And the latex gloves? I lead him down the corridor and send him tumbling onto my bed.

I show him my flat stomach, I want him to come on it. They're rotting behind the pantry. Wait for the whole family to finish dying, then off we go. The show begins: licking, clawing, writhing. But everything is tight, cold, tortured. Everything is that wallpaper of flowers and thorns. I try to inject some passion, we make love once. Twice. He's tired, his sciatica's troubling him. What the fuck is sciatica. He takes some painkillers. I'll bring you a glass of water with mint, the chlorophyll will do you good. The stifling world creeps into the room, once so full of magic. I leave him semi-erect on the mattress and walk naked into the hall. Mum's spying on us through the keyhole in the wardrobe door. I open it a crack. Was it ok? she asks. Shall I let you have one more or is it time? Did he kiss you with tongue? Make the most of it. Did you manage to…? Mum, you're gross. He has to make you come, the bastard. What are you on about? Great work with the rats, I was already running to find one. The house is silent. Nothing to suggest there's a naked man in the women's den. It's his fault for coming to a place like this. If he could stay like that for ten years in my bedroom, intact, always lying there on the bed, then everything would be beautiful and peaceful and I'd be only too happy to let him raise his little darlings. Take them into the fields to look for pineapples, boil crabs, splash in stagnant streams. His phone rings, and mum and I jump. Cover yourself up, will you? Your tits are distracting me, your nipples have grown so much, they're purple, God, they're larger than grandma's. Where did you come from. They're so dark. Are you really my daughter? Well, am I? Don't be an idiot. How could you not be, can't you see we're like a pea in a pod? Peas in a pod, mum. She passes me her blouse. We tiptoe towards the door, two ballerinas in tutus floundering around on the stage. He's whispering something, tender fatherly words. Pla pla pla, the couple say to each other. You're jealous, dear, that's what fucked up our life. I am not jealous. Yes you are, and I'm jealous of him too, and of women without children, jealous of a breeze, jealous of the world. Like cows after giving birth, a spongy thread is still hanging out of me, leaving a trail as I walk through the house. I put on a pair of knickers and hear him calling me, first whispering my name, then shouting it. It's time, says mum, he suspects something. Did he bring you the money? Shhhh, that doesn't matter now. Surely he has credit cards and debit cards too, maybe even cheques, vouchers. Can you forge his signature? Make him sign something for you. I suppose you want me to ask him for his PIN and passwords as well? Get him outside, I'll go out the other way, I'll take everything, you just need to bring him. Don't take too long, don't stay behind slobbering all over him. Be brief. A little bit longer and I'll go. You'll ruin everything for the tip of his cock and then he'll be hers forever. His taste, his eyes, all for her. Just a tiny bit longer. And in I go with the glass of water and the mint leaf.

Why are you getting dressed? It's late, if you want I'll give you a hand and then we can go for a drink in the bar by the river. But I'm giving you a drink now. Still, I need some fresh air. Let's go out into the garden then. Whatever you want. I thought you always liked seeing the boats go by, identifying the different engines. Well, yes, but that was before. You're still angry with me. No. Disappointed. No. Just because I'm having a child with her it doesn't mean… No, I get it. I couldn't deny her the opportunity, she was made for it, for motherhood, she's not like you. What am I like? You're gorgeous. Radiant. You're a different kind of woman, you're not a mother. She was a mother before she could walk. But honestly, having a child is nothing more than that, I'm telling you. I'd just received the most beautiful declaration of love I'd ever heard: having a child is nothing. And for the first time, he kissed me rather than me him, and again we were two heavenly bodies in space. Bewilderment. I almost forget mum's waiting by the henhouse with all the utensils ready. And I think, what an idiot, he drank all the water and I put nothing in it to send him to sleep, mum and I obviously haven't watched enough films. She'll have to be vicious, she'll have to thrust it through the tough skin. Mouths tasting of mint, and again I kiss him, and again.

I show him where I used to play when I was a girl. We're walking and he takes my hand. Mum must think she's hallucinating. We go into the cave where I used to hide when I was little to avoid seeing the old men castrating the animals or hanging them up by the hooves. I show him the lair where I spied on men bringing corpses down on sledges in the winter. The trench I hid in to make grenades and throw them. He takes an interest in my past, in that filthy fatherless hole. Like a scientist with thick glasses, he examines the trees I used to climb. For a second everything's back-to-front, the metal blade slicing my mother's flimsy spine in two. And then him and me eating dinner by candlelight, having kids who love to go high on the swings, smoking and blowing the smoke into the stars. I look over to where she's signalling frantically. A clucking sound catches his attention and he heads in that direction by himself, without me having to say anything stupid like how I simply must show him the vegetable patch. He walks, his long legs marking my lawn. He walks, distancing himself from my childhood. Later I'll kiss the soil and spend whole days stretched out on his footprints, madly in love. Mum's still standing on a stone bench behind the ivy, and he's facing the other way. The awning shields us from view, the adjacent doors, the swaying canopy of trees. I'm at the centre of everything. The psychotic gesture of the arm held high, the pointed elbow. The machete heavy like a child that needs protecting from a fall. Mother's eyes bulge. I can't give her the go-ahead, I can't nod, I can't lift my hand in a signal. But she doesn't need to be told. She hurls herself off the bench and gives that first blow with the knife to the back of the neck. And she topples him. That's when his eyes seek me out. I can still save him, make him my husband, the lord of the manor with jangling keys and a rifle. I can still have a go at being a good orphan. Sex is revolting. He's spitting blood and water now, his head inside out. Mother climbs on top of him. Get over here, for fuck's sake, she growls at me, get over here and do something. It's time to act but I'm paralysed. I can't do it, mum, I'm wearing spotty blue overalls and I'm too shy to enter the classroom. I can't even say my own name. Come here, dammit, and she passes it to me by the handle. It's heavy. I lift the machete with all my love, with all my dying heart. The rusty machete against the gloomy sky stabs him once in the stomach, again, she says, I lift it and let its weight fall on his chest, again, she says, and I lift it and sink the blade into his neck, and then, that's enough now, enough, show some mercy, take a deep breath, put it down now, let it go. Next to me there's a flat stone, I want to smash him with it hard, make his face go away. It's ok now, she says, you can rest.

What on earth is that. I don't mean to be crude but that thing looks like a gherkin, a horrible beauty. Let's have a look, oh yes, it is a bit odd, a fruit out of season, a vegetable lying in the sun. I never said anything to you, but now that I see his cock I think it's the key to the whole thing. Someone's watching me hungrily, it's sunny as well, I'm wearing patent leather shoes with little buckles and my fringe is over my eyes, parted in a cowlick. I'm wearing a checked skirt with pleats and I'm in fancy dress. Who's watching you, daughter dear? Something outside is watching me all through the party and afterwards too, when things start to fall, the tiny cups, the dainty china plates. Look, the gherkin's getting scorched, it's shrivelling, it's a courgette, a forkbeard fish, how funny. An interesting effect, like it's the first thing to go. An uncle, a neighbour, one of granny's men friends? Something was pulling at me, I could feel it in my tummy but you still sent me off to play on the back seat of the car. Could a person want something so badly they destroy it? I have this obsession with asking questions when I already know the answer. Asking like picking lice off a child's head and not stopping even when they're all gone and the boy's screaming, covered in vinegar, his head empty. Asking, knowing the answer, and stabbing a nail into the scalp. The first few times I saw you, when you'd just come out, you were immaculate, golden, your eyes green like an alien at certain times of day. When I went back to the hospital for a check-up, the nurses would call me over to congratulate me, the anaesthetists, the receptionists too, and I'd pull the blanket down a little so they could see how well put-together you were, how well-balanced you'd turned out. I wanted to show you off, but at the same time it was weird, like you weren't really mine, like I'd dialled the wrong number and got through to someone else. When I'd venture a few miles out of town with the pram, the two of us all alone and defenceless, I could have left you right there on the snowy road. Or on the beach. That's what I used to think. The tide carrying you off into the lightning. I would have done it if someone had promised me he'd come back. Like a hasty transaction at a militarised border. Something for you, something for me, and we go our separate ways. Like the mother who tells her young daughter, don't be such a simpleton. What's a better way of putting it? Not out of cruelty, I hope you understand, but so I could recover what I'd lost. There's no need, no need for you to explain anything at all. Now hug me, nice and tight. I gave birth to you, but you could just as well have given birth to me, don't you think?

Earlier we made love and nothing. Sometimes bodies are no more than intercourse, the product of intercourse. It's not happening, not working. Nothing's happening. Nothing. A final kiss, I take what's left of his face in my hands and smash a final kiss down on it. Eventually his phone rings and it drills through my mind. Like after a train crash, when people from the shanty towns clamber down to the tracks like monkeys and empty the pockets of the dying. Her waters have broken, she's losing it, she's waiting with open legs for him to come running. She needs his hands for the glutinous act. My love, she screams, my love, my darling. But those screams are nothing. I deserved him more than she did. He was mine, not hers, she just trapped him with her reproductive organs. Mum and I exchange glances, she gives me the go-ahead and I smash the phone to bits. I hope it gets strangled by the cord. I hope it gets stuck. The hens are prowling around, anticipating a feast. The foxes and stags will come down the path later for their share. There's enough for everyone, suck up the scraps. Cop a feel, you beasts. We're innocent. We're the real victims, Your Honour. And at last the moment comes when he's no longer breathing, like looking at a lover one day and realising you feel nothing. A silence made of crackling and buzzing descends on us like a downpour. He was an arrogant swine, says mother. A brute with no principles, I add. A coward, all in all, nothing but a coward. Mine a bourgeois asshole, yours an unreliable letch. A waste of space, the pair of them. But in this life we reap what we sow, and she yanks the words out of my mouth. He was so so so beautiful it was actually disgusting, mummy. The sound of small aeroplanes flying above us and swooping down. We could taxi along the motorway between the windmills and the river. Get a bird's eye view of him all scrambled up. Animal instincts, earth, sex, it all comes back gradually, like the taste buds of an ex-smoker. I lift my head to the sun and take myself by the neck. Leaving no note. For once. Good news, mum, I've hanged myself. We spend the afternoon examining his body. You've finally stopped harassing him, she observes.

Midnight comes and everything's clean and ready to go. The table set up for a game of canasta. Soft music in the air and the whole room seems to be dancing. Mum walks past in an apron, chicken wings and dip on a tray. I serve the drinks. At the sound of the cork, she shivers. The grass freshly mown. The henhouse shut. No utensils in sight, no scars, no slashed-out earth. Everything in its place, new clothes, the others hanging on the line. Cheers, to us, I say, watching the horizon as it swallows us up. She nods. Like we're in a fancy restaurant, only alone. The money safely hidden, the keys to the new car on the table. Not for nothing did we break our backs working, she says suddenly. Itching to try out the sliding sunroof down some country roads. Itching to soak up the smog in the big-city suburbs. Itching for an ATM, a quick visit to a hiking shop, and the tank filled up in the most remote petrol station. Mother with oven gloves, leaning over to serve me, I'm ten years old and she's a grandma with saggy tits dishing up chicken and onions. In a few days we'll have hundreds of tomatoes, we can offer some to our neighbours. Absolutely, I say, and bake something for them too while we're at it, strawberry pies, we can take them round while they're still warm. Yes, definitely, with brown sugar on top. We were talking like we were being spied on or the telephone was bugged. We discussed how we'd rearrange the house, divide up the chores, pay our debts, our taxes, how we'd try to get involved in local community projects. How we'd try to fit in. We talked without looking at each other. Maybe we could start taking care of the terminally ill, donate clothes to charity shops, give our time to people who really need it. Let's begin with the autistic, she said, full of enthusiasm. Let's give haircuts to the disabled, I added. And I have no idea how we didn't burst out laughing.

The cutlery crossed, the chicken bones sucked clean, the rims of the glasses smeared with saliva, everything stacked up and ready to be devoured by repetition. We're chatting in the kitchen, the sink overflowing with washing-up foam, I pass her the plates and she envelopes them in the tea towel when suddenly we hear a noise. We freeze. And another noise, clearer now. Footsteps, says mum. A thief. Someone's trying to break in. To climb through a window. Mother drops the tea towel and leaves the room. I peer at the front path through the keyhole. She comes back with the car keys and we make for the door. A window in the neighbour's house is lit up, unusually. But no one looks out. Someone's said something, let's get out of here, mum hisses, no time to pack a bag. Grab the cash. What? I'm surprised to find that I don't want to leave him. I don't want to move away from him, not even a short distance. Not even for a night. Maybe this is stupid but I'm only just realising, I want to spend the rest of my life with him, mummy. And do you think this is the right time for declarations of love? Do you want me to call in the priest to pronounce you husband and wife? I'm never moving away, and if one day I have a child – I fall silent. Mother, I want to have his child. You should have thought of that sooner, my dear. I'm afraid you're screwed now. If I ever have a child it'll be next to this mound, and my son will play around his smell. Yes, he'll love his smell. He'll look up to him, he'll make the grass grow. Are you quite finished? And when he enters the years of dread, I'll dig with my own nails. I'm not coming, mum. You go on your own. Don't worry, I'll wait for you here, and I see his shoes lined up next to ours. We'll wait for you. But mother pushes me outside, this is no time for lovers' tiffs. Someone witnessed the scene, someone knows, do you understand? Get in, and she gives me a shove. And get in is once when I was eight and we were going camping, and all the way there I looked out of the window at the street lights trying to electrocute me. My fingers poised to pull the door handle, imagining how I'd tumble into the ditch, seeing myself coil up as soon as I was free, calculating the force I'd need for the moment the car slowed down. Mum was singing at the wheel and even though I never took my fingers off the handle, I didn't open the door. Coming, I said. May you rest in peace in your grave, my love. And we left without turning on the headlights.

We're on the road and everything's so black, so lonely, so true, like eagles flying blind and crashing into a rockface. Were we mistaken? There's no one around. The neighbour's light is off. Was it on before or did we imagine it? Let's drive for a bit just in case, then head back and board up the doors. Mum, we're in the countryside. So what. It's a tiny village of run-down geriatrics in the middle of fucking nowhere. Still, you never know with geriatrics. The car doing fifteen miles an hour like an animal heading for the chop. Just as we're circling back, ready to return to the bedsheets, the moths and one last cold beer, we see something flash past in front of us. A quick thing made of air, it moved but it didn't look like legs. You saw that, right? Did it have two legs? I couldn't tell. Mum speeds up, the engine cuts through the hypnosis. We pull into the industrial park.

We drive straight over the roundabout. A police car hidden behind a small cluster of trees flashes its lights a few times, an arm waving out of the window, an order. I can imagine the faces of the young police officers, they must have been waiting to run into a pair like us in the middle of the night ever since they graduated. Mum, stop the car, stop the car. But the chase has begun, and mother speeds up the ramp to the car park. Mother's playing roadrunner, eating vitamins and pieces of fruit like Pac-Man. She doesn't dodge the road signs and now she's going the wrong way down a side street towards the river. Are the bastards still after us? Yes, mum, they're still there. What did you expect them to do, give up and go fishing? They'll see, they're going to pay for this, mark my words. It has to come to us at some point. What has to come to us? I don't want it, whatever it is. Have you ever won anything in your whole fucking life? No? Well then, it's about time. Hold on tight and open the roof. Fancy car, this. Mother skids over the ditch and the stones clatter everywhere like broken glass. The birds and tadpoles flee. And I can't think about anything else. My brain no longer feels like mine. There's no way we'll still be alive in an hour, so I hold on tight and scream and hit her with my fist but I do it hopelessly, pointlessly.

Empty of desire. I look at everything without saying goodbye, but I'm no longer in this world. No images flash before my eyes, I don't know what being alive was about. There was no childhood, no riddle solved, no word of respite, only stifling rooms and the smell inside her shoes. The car jolts along, colliding with old houses, flowerbeds, machinery. Leaves fall on us, tree trunks. The car shaking us, full speed into what, into where, mother still going, foot to the floor. Are they still behind us, are they catching up? I turn to see but the pressure makes my head very heavy, my head turns into a helmet, my brain long gone. We lay waste to everything, blows to the roof, blows to the windows, until we're brought to a halt by a huge ball of interlocking branches. The car jerks back and forth and gets stuck in the swarm. Buzzing. Cheep cheep. Mother crawls out on her hands and knees and cuts her face in two on the splinters. I drag myself out, roll on the ground, gashes criss-cross my skin. We're in one piece, covered in blood. Let it all explode, let it all turn to dust, says mother, still wanting more.

Director & Editor: Carolina Orloff
Director: Samuel McDowell

charcopress.com

Feebleminded was published on
90gsm Munken Premium Cream paper.

The text was designed using Bembo 11.5 and ITC Galliard.

Printed in February 2019 by TJ International
Padstow, Cornwall, PL28 8RW